To Charlie Gillespie, those shoulders, and that
smile.

This one is loosely based on you and Luke.

Sorry?

PROLOGUE

sh Kane was aware he was a disappointment to his parents. Instead of applying to college to study for a high-powered career the way they'd wanted him to, he spent his days busking outside a coffee shop not far from Mulholland.

Growing up in L.A., Ash was surrounded by people wanting to be famous, be it in movies, on TV, or whatever. He didn't want to necessarily be famous; he just wanted his music to be known. Wanted to leave a legacy behind for people to be able to relate to.

Ever since his mom and dad had bought him his first guitar for his sixth birthday, he'd been obsessed with music. Not only was it the escape he sometimes needed, but it had brought him the three best friends a musician could ever want.

Chris, Wes, and Joey had the same dreams as he did – well, Joey wanted the fame and fortune he thought their music would bring them and Chris wanted the girls – but their main drive was the music itself.

The others were still in their senior year of high school, so during the day he was alone. His dad kept ragging on him to get a job if he wasn't going to college, but Ash didn't want to be tied down to someone else's schedule. Instead, he spent the majority of his time with his guitar in his hand, an old mic, and one of his beanies on the floor in front of him. Not only was he making money, but he was also away from his parents and their incessant nagging.

He'd only been there an hour, but he'd already made more money than he would have working a minimum wage job that ate into his rehearsal time with the boys. He sang a mixture of his own songs and covers, knowing that hearing songs people knew would make them stop and listen to him, especially the tourists. Maybe they'd drop some change into his hat.

As passing trade had slowed for a moment, a

small quirk curled his top lip as he turned his body to look through the window of the brightly lit coffee house. His fingers strummed the opening notes of an Ed Sheeran cover. She was working again, the one who seemed to hate the music he performed, the one he'd overhead complaining about his song choices on the phone to someone.

At first it had annoyed him, and he'd been tempted to justify his choices before moving onto his spot down at the pier, but for some reason he didn't. With mischief on his mind, he made sure that the more she moaned, the more he played songs by artists she loathed. It was petty he knew, but it gave him a sort of perverse pleasure seeing her beautiful face scrunch up whenever she heard a song she didn't like.

It was the little things that brightened his days. Naturally, he never mentioned any of this to his band mates, not if he didn't want to be teased relentlessly about it. But as she caught his gaze now through the window and scowled, he could feel the satisfaction zip through his body and he turned back around and belted out the song like he was on stage.

sh pulled his beaten-up Chevy up in the lot outside his old high school and waited for his friends. As music played softly from the radio, which was always tuned to an old 90s station, he rested his journal on the steering wheel and scribbled some lyrics down before he forgot them.

"Hey, man, how did it go today?" Chris' voice made Ash jump as the first of his friends climbed into the car that had their band's logo spray painted onto the hood. *Rare Breed* had been together for almost three years, and while they were playing gigs, it wasn't enough. Not for Ash at least. While the rest of the guys were still in school, they had other things to worry about.

"Not bad, bro, I got over a hundred dollars. I'm gonna use it to get more shirts printed for our gig next week, making sure these ones don't fall apart in the rain." Chris blushed. He'd been the one to get their first shirts made up and had made the mistake of going to the cheapest place he'd found online.

"Sweet. I *love* seeing girls wearing our shirts." Chris' green eyes lit up at the thought of girls wearing a tee with their band name on. He was girl mad – then again, at almost eighteen, what high school senior wasn't? He flirted with every female with a pulse, but often lucked out. The blame was almost always placed squarely on his bright red hair; pale, freckly skin; and the fact he was just over six feet tall and pretty skinny. Ash had often been subjected to a rant about Chris' defective DNA when he struck out with a pretty girl.

Thanks to YouTube and Instagram, Rare Breed had a small following of fans who showed up to their shows in homemade shirts and who knew the words to all their songs. It blew them all away, and it was a start to their music careers. But as always, it was never enough.

The back doors of Ash's car opened at the

same time as Wes and Joey climbed in. Ash fired up the engine and peeled out of the lot, the tires squealing against the warm asphalt.

:: ::

The guys rehearsed in the old garage behind Joey's house. Joey grabbed them all a soda and some potato chips and then they carried on working on a song they'd started the week before.

After three hours of rehearsals, Ash drove Wes and Chris home before going home himself. It wasn't late so his mom and dad would still be up and waiting for him.

"That you, son?" His dad called out from the living room as Ash let himself in. He asked the same question every time Ash came home, despite him being an only child, and his mom – the only other person who lived there – being sat with him knitting as his dad watched the TV.

"Yeah, it's me." He walked in, pulling his beanie off his head.

"Have a good day, honey?" his mom asked, smiling up at him.

"It was okay."

He knew his parents loved him, although

they may not agree with some of the life choices he was making, which was more than his friends could say. He just wished sometimes that his mom wasn't so... smothering at times. Yeah, it was great she showed an interest in the things he did, but sometimes he wished she would just let him live his life.

"That's great. There's a plate of food in the oven keeping warm for you."

With a smile, Ash bent over and kissed his mom's cheek. "Thanks. I'm starving."

He hadn't wanted to break into his day's earnings to buy more than a cheap street dog, loaded with the works. His stomach growled loudly, making both his parents laugh. "I'd better go get that food," he said, heading toward the kitchen. He pulled his warm plate of meatloaf out of the oven and climbed up onto the counter to eat it while scrolling through his phone to see if there had been any activity on the band's Instagram account. They all had access to it and posted random photos and videos to it intermittently, so Ash never knew what he was going to find when he checked it. On more than one occasion, there had been sneakily taken photos of him shirtless backstage at gigs that Chris posted in their stories or short videos of him dicking about on karaoke which he'd only done once.

According to Wes, their female fans *loved* seeing him like that. Insisted that not only his muscular shoulders drove them mad and that Ash was the main reason many of them came to their shows. Ash wasn't sure how to deal with that, so tried not to think about it too often. He wasn't in Rare Breed to find a life partner, but as long as people turned up to their shows and liked their music, what did it matter why they'd bought a ticket in the first place?

After washing up his empty plate, Ash poured himself a glass of milk and went up to his bedroom. Once he closed the door behind him, he felt at peace. His green guitar case was placed in its usual spot on his desk as he shucked off his Chucks and sat on his bed, his journal in front of him. He drank his milk as he read over what he'd been working on in his car, but none of it seemed to work. He pulled a pen out of the back pocket of his jeans and scratched out all but one line.

I see you through my own reflection.

Before he could do any more, there was a soft tap on his window. When he turned his head to look at the glass, Chris' pale face looked in at him. Scrambling across his bed, Ash opened the window allowing his friend to climb into his room.

"Thanks, man." Chris kicked off his combat boots, and hung his jacket on the back of Ash's chair as he dropped his backpack next to it. He pulled the air bed out from under Ash's bed. It was never deflated these days, and Ash's mom always made sure there was a clean blanket and a couple of pillows in Ash's room for it.

"Rough night?" Ash asked his friend.

"The roughest. I'm exhausted." Chris scrubbed a hand over his face.

He stripped down to his boxers and climbed into the bed that was always available to him. Within minutes, he was asleep. Ash watched as the stress on his friend's face faded away. Quietly, Ash flicked his lamp off so he wouldn't disturb Chris. He could still see the page in front of him by the light filtering through from the landing outside his open bedroom door.

:: ::

After driving Chris to school and asking Wes and Joey to keep an eye on him, Ash drove over to the studio. Walking through the side gate and around the back of the house felt as natural as breathing to him. They'd all escaped to the large garage Joey's dad had tried to convert unsuccessfully for them at one time or another. Ash mostly to write and feel like he could breathe away from his parent's pointed looks and comments, Chris to get away from the house that hadn't been a home in years, Wes to be able to just be himself, and Joey to have some peace away from his three younger sisters.

As he walked into the studio space, a feeling of peace washed over Ash. There was something about the way the light filtered through the windows that always made him not only grateful to be alive, but to have a purpose in life. Music flowed through his veins as much as the blood that sustained his body. He just wished his parents understood that more; neither of them seemed to have ever had a dream to chase. But this week had been a good one with them, and he wasn't going to let that change anytime soon.

Dropping his bag on the floor, he sank onto the couch his dad had got at a flea market just for this space, back when they thought music was only a hobby. He leaned back and allowed his eyes to close. Silence invaded every aspect of his being for the five minutes Ash could put up with. When it got too oppressive, he moved over to the stereo, connected it to his phone and pressed play on his favorite 90s playlist. Low volume music filled the air around him as he sat back down and pulled his journal out of his backpack.

Before turning back to the half-finished song from the night before, he flicked to the very last page and checked out the rough timetable he'd scribbled down. The girl at the coffee shop was working the late shift, so he had a few hours to get some work done.

2

Sound check had gone well for their gig in a small café on a side street near downtown L.A. It wasn't the best venue, and by the time *Rare Breed* hit the stage, it wasn't even half full of customers. But the ones who were there seemed to enjoy their set if they're nodding their heads and tapping their feet to the beat was any indication. Three songs at the beginning of the play bill wasn't exactly what Ash had in mind when he'd signed them up, but it was better than nothing. It was all about the exposure and they needed all they could get.

By the time he'd unhooked his gear and climbed down off stage, the rest of the guys were already chatting to a couple of girls – well, Joey and Chris were, fighting over who got the most attention – trying to get them to buy a copy of the demo they'd paid to have produced semi-professionally and a t-shirt. Wes was behind them, an amused smile on his face. From where he stood, Ash couldn't help but laugh. Chris' red hair was dulled by the dim lighting and Joey's dirty blond hair looked as dark as Wes'. The height difference between them also made it look more comical. Chris towered over Joey, who was a bit sensitive about his short stature. Ash couldn't understand why it bothered him so much, they were the same height. With a grin on his face, he moved across the room to join his friends.

"Well, boys, that could have been worse," he stated once the girls had left, splitting the cost of a CD between them.

"Yeah, there could have been no girls," Chris and Joey spoke in unison as they went out to load their gear into Joey's dad's van they always borrowed for shows.

"You guys need to seriously assess your priorities." Wes tutted at them as he pulled his phone out of the fanny pack that always slung around his waist. He'd been over the moon when they'd come back into fashion – not that he'd ever stopped wearing it. "There's more to life than girls."

"Only a gay man comfortable in his sexuality could say that," Joey snarked, earning him a slap to the chest from Ash. "What?"

"Rein your mouth in."

"Chill, man. I was just making a statement."

Ash had often wondered if Joey had issues with Wes's sexuality. Their keyboard player often passed what could be seen as snarky remarks about Wes not being into girls, but always played it off as a joke when either Chris or Ash pulled him up on them. Wes, he noticed, never said anything, often choosing to engross himself in something else until it was all over. Not that he could be blamed, considering how his parents treated him.

"Yeah, don't, bro. It's not cool," Ash snapped at him as he grabbed his acoustic and made his way over to his car, Chris behind him. "I'll see you guys tomorrow at the studio."

"He's getting worse, man." Chris said as Ash followed Joey and Wes and the van out of the tiny lot behind the venue.

"Yeah, I know. I don't know what to do about him."

"Does he know?" Ash looked at Chris out of the corner of his eye as he navigated his car along the ever-busy roads home.

"About what?" Now wasn't the time to play dumb, but he couldn't help it.

"You know what." Chris pinned him with a stare that felt as if it were seeing straight through him.

"No, he doesn't. And he never will, right?" As they turned a corner, Ash took the opportunity to take his eyes off the road to pin his friend with a look. "Whatever happened between me and Wes is in the past. We've both moved on. Joey doesn't need to know everything about us all."

"Okay, I get it." Chris held his hands up in surrender.

:: ::

Ash lay on his bed listening to Chris snoring. He'd already sent Wes a text to see if he was okay and had a response in the positive that he wasn't sure he believed. Wes seemed to forget exactly how well Ash knew him. Closing his eyes, he let his mind drift away into memories that had been dredged up on the drive home.

Always knowing he was different to Chris and Joey; Ash hadn't quite worked out he was bi. Yeah, he'd had girlfriends at school; nothing serious because they hated coming second best to his music, but he often found himself checking out guys too. It didn't bother him because hey, 21st century and all that.

It had been when Wes turned up at his house that night almost a year ago, his dark-brown eyes red from crying, and Ash had wrapped him in a tight hug, slowly managing to get his friend to speak to him that he realized he wasn't completely straight himself.

"I need to tell you something and I need you to be okay with me after."

"Wes, I'll always be all right with you. You're one of my best friends and nothing you can say to me will ever change that."

Wes took hold of Ash's hand and squeezed it as if he was scared he was going to float away or something. After a few minutes of almost silence, he took a deep breath and finally spoke.

"I'm gay." The fear in his voice was painfully obvious to Ash. His best friend was terrified to tell

him the truth about himself and that hurt more than his hiding who he really was.

"I know." If Wes was going to be completely honest, then so was he.

"Are you okay wit- wait, what?" Wes ran his hands through his long hair that matched his eyes, a nervous habit he'd never been able to shift.

"I know. I've known for forever. You're not exactly subtle about it, especially when you check guys out." He grinned at Wes hoping to relax him. It didn't quite work even if some of the tension left his friend's shoulders.

"And it doesn't bother you?"

"Why would it?"

"Well..." Wes didn't have a response. The sigh that escaped him as Ash wrapped him up in another hug was loud.

"Who else have you told?"

"No one, just you." Ash was honored his friend trusted him so much. "I want to tell Chris and Joey, but I can't tell my mom and dad, not yet."

"What about Lizzie?" Wes' younger sister, Elizabeth, was a year younger than him and absolutely idolized him.

"I don't know."

"You know she'd accept you even if you told her you were an alien impostor. You'll need someone at home on your side if you ever do tell them."

"Maybe. Can I stay here tonight?"

"Sure." Wes crawled off Ash's bed and onto the airbed and passed out pretty much straight away. Ash sat up, leaning against the headboard, missing the physical contact with Wes. As his mind turned over, he grabbed his journal and a pen.

It had been just after that night he and Wes had begun a tentative relationship. The only people who knew were Chris and Lizzie, they were the only ones who'd completely accepted Wes and the two of them being a thing. Joey, who had taken a few days to reassure everyone he was cool with the news that Wes was gay, hadn't noticed at all, and that suited everyone.

It fizzled out after three or so months as they both realized they were better as friends, but Ash knew he'd always hold a special place in his heart for Wes for the rest of his life. It was through this boy's strength Ash came out as bi. No fanfare, no sitting people down. He just announced it the only way he knew how to. Bluntly.

He was lucky. His mom and dad were cool with his sexuality, even if they didn't completely understand it. He appreciated them so much for that, especially after Wes' dad referred to his son as 'the family fag' for three weeks after finally being told the truth. His mom hadn't really said much to him at all, despite Lizzie trying to keep them civil. Wes had spent more time at Ash's house than anywhere else, making their friend-ship stronger than ever.

Chris snorted in his sleep, making Ash's mind let go of the past and brought him straight back into the present. Yeah, Joey couldn't ever find out about him and Wes. Not because either of them was ashamed, but because Joey was a bit of a dick, which was becoming more and more obvious the more attention *Rare Breed* received.

3

S etting his mic stand up outside *Downtown Beans*, Ash could see the cute barista smiling at customers as she served them. Her entire face lit up when she smiled, and the customers seemed to genuinely like her from what he could see.

"Have you not gone in to speak to her yet?" Wes' voice made him jump. Ash hadn't seen his friend walk along the sidewalk toward him.

"What are you talking about?"

"You've been playing outside this place every day for almost a month now rather than down by the pier. I knew there had to be a reason for the sudden change. Now I know." He waggled his brows. "So the question is are you going to grow some balls to go in there and speak to her?" Wes looked through the window as Ash distracted himself by connecting his acoustic to the small amp he always brought with him and dropping his beanie in front of the stand.

"It's a great tourist trap, that's the only reason." Even to himself, his excuse sounded weak. He couldn't even remember why he started playing here in the first place.

"Sure, bro." Without saying anything else, Wes entered the coffee shop before he could be stopped. Feeling panic rise, Ash turned his back to the window and began to play his favorite Green Day track, losing himself almost instantly in the melody.

Good Riddance was one of the most beautiful songs Ash had ever learned by another artist, and he loved singing it. It gave him the chance to show the deepness and husky quality to his voice.

His singing filled the air and a few passers-by stopped to listen, making him smile as they dropped a couple of dollar bills into his hat. It was always a crowd favorite and usually gener-ated people giving him money as they sang along.

By the time he finished the song to applause, Wes still hadn't come back. As he messed with the tuning on his guitar, Ash looked through the window, watching Wes and the barista chatting.

This was exactly why he hadn't invited the guys to play with him here. All he needed was for Chris and Joey to show up and work things out too. That would be *outstanding,* and he would be hearing about the barista for months. He looked both ways on the sidewalk to make sure they weren't doing just that, but there was no sign of them. With a sigh of relief, he began his next song, a Rare Breed original.

As he sang, Wes came out holding two takeout cups, placing one for Ash on his amp. He stood back to watch Ash do what he was best at. As if he couldn't resist, he was soon beating a drum beat on his chest and legs with his hands and harmonizing with his lead singer, which caused Ash to grin widely at him.

When they finished, they high-fived and Ash picked up the now almost cold drink Wes had brought out for him.

"So... her name's Camille, she's a student, and she hates 90s alt rock."

"I knew that last one." Ash was grateful to Wes for finding out information for him, information he was too much of a chicken to find out for himself.

"Let me guess, you play a lot of 90s alt rock when she's working?"

"Maybe."

Wes rolled his eyes. "Bro, you got it bad for a girl you've never spoken to."

"Dude, I do not have it bad. I just like getting a reaction."

"Ashley Kane, you do indeed have it bad. You forget I know you and your facial expressions. Why won't you go and speak to her? She's nice."

Ash couldn't answer that, so he decided to play another song. He drained the last of his coffee, dropping the empty cup into the nearest trash can before launching into the instantly recognizable opening riff to Nirvana's *Come as You Are*. Wes rolled his eyes again, said his good-byes, and walked away.

:: ::

When he got to the studio, only Joey was

there, restringing his electric. His dirty blond hair hung over his face as he concentrated. Ash dropped his bag on the floor at his feet and made his way up the rickety stairs to a mezzanine loft that he always worried would collapse whenever he went up there.

"I broke my damn G-string."

Naturally, Ash snorted.

"Fuck you, bro. Fuck you."

Ash couldn't help laughing out loud as he unpacked his own electric that was always stored up in the loft. He preferred his acoustic, but the electric worked better with their sound, especially on stage.

"Where're the guys?"

"Chris is in chatting to my dad and I don't know where Wes is." Ash couldn't help but smile at the thought of Chris spending time with Joey's dad. Tristan was pretty cool, a bit of a hippy, but cool nonetheless. Seeing as his own dad had no time for him, even more so when his older brother moved away, Chris spent as much time with Joey's and Ash's dads as he could. They both loved him as if he was their own and understood what he needed from their interactions.

"I'll go in and say hey before we get started. You continue fiddling with your G-string." Ash dodged the ball cap that was thrown at him as he ducked through the huge doors and made his way through the yard into the kitchen.

"Hey, bro, how did it go today?" Chris was sat at the breakfast bar as Tristan typed away on his laptop.

"It was okay. I put in the order for some more shirts yesterday too. Fifty of them this time, and hopefully better quality."

"Dude, let it go." Chris' cheeks flushed red as they did every time anyone reminded him about the cheap shirts he'd ordered. Feeling a little guilty, Ash wrapped an arm around him and apologized.

"You ready to rehearse?"

"Sure. See ya, Tristan."

Joey's dad waved a hand in response without looking up from his work.

Wes still wasn't in the studio, so the three of them played a few older songs of theirs, not wanting to work on anything new without their drummer. As they packed away, the blond ran into the studio, panting.

"I'm so sorry, guys. I was down at the pier and completely lost track of time. Did I miss anything?" He looked at Ash in particular, knowing he wrote the majority of their songs and almost always had something new for them.

"Nah, man. We just jammed for a bit."

"Oh, great." His shoulders sagged as he relaxed at Ash's words. "I am sorry though, and I'll make sure I make the next rehearsal."

"Seriously, don't worry about it," Chris told him, putting his hand on Wes' shoulder. "Anyway, I gotta book. Dad's working nights this week, so I can get some sleep tonight." With a last round of fist bumps, Chris left to go home.

"Yeah, I got some homework to finish up. I'll catch you guys later." Joey left the studio, leaving Wes and Ash alone.

Sinking onto the couch, Ash pulled Wes to sit next to him.

"So, what got you so distracted today?" His friend didn't say anything for a while and Ash could see him trying to work out what to say. "Hey, did you meet someone?" he asked, keeping his voice soft.

"I... I think so."

"Bro, that's fantastic. Tell me about him."

For the next hour, the friends sat on a couch and the light outside dimmed, as Ash listened to his ex-boyfriend rave about the cute surfer he'd met down at the beach.

4

Once again, Ash was outside *Downtown Beans* watching Camille work. He hadn't planned on setting up that day, but his acoustic was still strapped to his back – he pretty much went everywhere with it anyway and didn't always trust leaving it in his car. Today was the day he was going to go inside. He was going to talk to her, and he was going to make her laugh the way Wes had. He turned his back on the window and almost chickened out. As he began to walk away, his phone chimed from the pocket of his jeans.

Go inside Ashley.

A text from Wes. Ash looked around, wondering if his friend was watching him from somewhere, but saw no sign of his floppy hair. Readjusting the beanie on his head, he took a deep breath and pushed the door open. Instantly, the aroma of fresh coffee assaulted his senses as he approached the counter. To his horror, Camille was nowhere to be seen. Instead, a tall and muscular blond kid was serving the customers in front of him. Feeling let down, he debated leaving and trying another day, but decided to grab a drink anyway.

Brian - according to his name badge - took his order without making eye contact, which suited Ash. Once he picked up the steaming cup, he walked through the shop and found an empty table to sit at. He pulled his guitar off, standing it against the wall, and sat down, pulling his journal and a pen out of the front pocket of his guitar bag.

Scribbling out words and correcting himself in the journal, Ash sipped at his coffee, completely absorbed in his work. The sounds of the coffee shop around him had faded and all he could hear was the melody floating around in his mind.

"Hey, do you need a top up?" A female voice asked from the side of him. Blinking away the song, Ash looked up to see Camille smiling down at him.

"Uh…" Feeling like an idiot, Ash cleared his throat and tried again. "Sorry, bit distracted."

"Yeah, you've been sat there nursing the same cup for over an hour." Camille smiled down at him again. "It's either empty or stone cold. Top up?"

"Sure, that would be great, thanks."

Camille leaned over him to grab his cup, invading his senses with her hair and perfume. She smelled of flowers and coffee, an intoxicating mix. Before he managed to shake his head clear, she was walking away from him toward the counter. Rather than watch her like a creep, he turned his attention back to his journal. The song was almost finished, but was still missing something, something he couldn't put his finger on.

"Here you go. Black, one sugar, right?" Camille was back, holding out a steaming cup. Ash took it from her, not missing the fact their fingers brushed together. Swallowing the lump in his throat, he smiled up at her.

"Thanks, how did you know?"

"Brian told me your last order before he finished his shift."

Looking around, he saw that other than two girls at a table in the corner, he and Camille were the only people in the room. And it was almost dark outside. Glancing at his watch told him it was his turn to miss rehearsal with the guys. He knew he should leave and head back, but he didn't want to leave, not just yet.

"How much do I owe for the coffee?" He pulled his wallet out of his guitar bag and pulled a ten out and handed it to her.

"I'll just go get your change."

"Keep it." He grinned at her, noticing a slight blush to her skin that wasn't completely unpleasant to look at.

"Th- thanks," she stuttered slightly before turning and going back to the counter. He watched her for a moment, sipping at his coffee before turning his attention back to the journal on the table in front of him. Ash was feeling pretty good about himself and couldn't quite shift the smile from his face.

:: ::

Humming, Ash let himself into the house.

"Someone's in a good mood," his mom

commented as he dumped his stuff at the bottom of the stairs.

"Hey, Mom, I'm great. How was your day?" His mom worked at a physician's office and often had crazy stories about some of the patients, whom she never named, and their complaints.

"Busy. I'm just heading up to bed, but I saved you some dinner." She kissed him on the cheek before climbing the stairs. Ash walked into the den where his dad was sitting in his chair watching an old black and white movie.

"Hey, son."

"Hey, Dad. What you watching?" Ash sat on the large couch and watched the pictures move on the TV for a few minutes.

"Nothing in particular. It's mainly background noise while I read." He held up the book Ash hadn't noticed he was holding. "Hey, are you okay?"

"Yeah, why?"

"You have a look on your face I can't read." His parents and friends always joked that if ever any of them wanted to know what Ash was thinking, all they had to do was look at his face. He was an open book apparently.

"I'm cool. I've just been busy working on a new song."

"Yeah? What's this one about?" Ash's dad put his book face down on the table and turned to face his son. It wasn't often either of his parents showed an interest in his music, but when they did, it gave him a warm feeling of acceptance.

"Er... it's kinda about a girl."

"Oh, tell me about her?"

Ash took a deep breath and began speaking. As he reached the end of his short story, he saw his dad smiling widely at him.

"What?" he asked, confused.

"Nothing. You just look happy." He felt his face heat up at his dad's words. "It's good to see."

"Yeah, thanks. I'm gonna go and get my food, then head upstairs and try to finish this song before showing it to the guys tomorrow."

"Night, son." His dad picked his book back up and was instantly engrossed. Ash envied his dad for his love of reading, but he'd never found a book that held his attention long enough before it gave him an idea for a song.

"Night," he said softly, getting up and walking upstairs without even getting his plate of food.

:: ::

Weekends, if they didn't have a show, were spent in the studio working on new music. While Ash was their main songwriter, the other guys often wrote songs that they played. By the time Ash had the courage to show them his newest song, they'd already been practicing for three hours.

"So... I have something new I've been working on for a few days. It's pretty much finished, but I think it's missing something, and I can't work out what."

"Play it for us, and we'll work it out together," Wes suggested.

Ash put his pick between his teeth as he flicked through the pages of the journal until he found the right page. Then he began to play, singing softly.

Watching you ignoring me
Through the glass of life
Your hips swaying as you walk
Not noticing me noticing you

Watching you from the doorway

I can't keep my eyes away
Your lips parting as you talk
Not noticing me noticing you

"Bro, that's an amazing ballad. Who's it about?" Chris asked as Joey grabbed his ringing phone, climbed out from behind his keyboard, and slipped out of the door of the garage without giving one word of explanation about the fact he was leaving. Chris raised a brow as he watched Joey depart and then turned his attention back to Ash.

"No one in particular. Been doing a lot of people watching this past week." He didn't make eye contact with Wes. He knew if he did, Wes would be looking at him wearing a smug grin.

"Cool. Well, I can't see what you think's missing, but I'm not the insane perfectionist you are. I'm gonna go grab snacks from the house and see what Joey's doing." Chris put his bass on its stand, and practically danced out through the doors Joey had left open.

Awkwardness washed over Ash once he was left alone with Wes.

"It's about her, isn't it? Camille at *Downtown Beans*?" The drummer stepped down from behind his kit and walked over to Ash, who was still not looking directly at his friend. "You really like her, don't you?"

"I don't even *know* her," Ash protested, standing his acoustic on the stand and collapsing onto his favorite couch. "How can you like someone you don't know?"

Wes sat next to him and took hold of one of his hands. Ash looked down at his calloused fingers and compared them to his ex's large, strong ones.

"Ash, attraction isn't based on how well you know someone, just how much their appearance appeals to you in a number of ways. Besides, you can always get to know her."

Hanging his head so his chin hit his chest, Ash let out a long exhale. He was screwed.

5

Ash sat at his regular table in the coffee house. He'd been going inside before setting up outside for the past couple of weeks and was starting to get to know the staff and regular customers. He always had his journal in front of him as there was something about the atmosphere that seemed to inspire him in a way he'd never experienced before.

"Hey, music man. How's it going?" Leah, one of the part-time baristas, walked in, making sure to stop at his table for a quick chat as she did most days she worked.

"Hey, Leah. How's college?" It was crazy how well he'd got to know these people in two weeks. He knew Brian was on a sports scholarship and played college football, Leah was studying business management so she could work as an agent or manager for musicians, and Camille... well, he'd been blown away when he found out she was studying music. According to Leah, who happened to be her best friend and roommate, the girl had an amazing voice and was an insane songwriter. He'd wanted to talk to Camille about it, but she'd not been in since he'd found out, due to having a project due.

"Crazy busy, but I'm loving every minute of it."

"Gnarly." Ash was glad he hadn't gone to college, he didn't have the attention span for studying even though he loved to learn, plus it would have eaten into his music time.

"Very. I best get to work." She started to walk away but turned back as she rummaged through her backpack. "Oh, thought you might be interested in this." She handed him a piece of paper.

Looking down, the neon colors on the flyer advertising an open mic night on campus hurt his eyes. He looked back up, flashing her a wide smile, and giving her the thumbs up.

Open mic nights were common in Los Angeles, where everyone wanted to be spotted and to get famous, but he and the guys had never done one. They preferred shows where they could sing more than one song, but maybe they could get the students interested in their music this way. He pulled his phone out of his pocket, about to message the band when Wes walked in, followed by a guy who could only be the surfer he'd met down at the pier.

"Hey, Ash." His friend looked almost embarrassed as they joined him at his table.

"Hey, Wes, and…?" He turned to the surfer. His sun-bleached blond hair was tied up in a messy knot showing off the sharp lines of his face. Ash could see what attracted Wes to him.

"Sorry, this is Wyatt. Wyatt, this is Ash."

"Nice to meet you, heard a lot about you." Wyatt held his hand out for Ash to shake.

"Well, don't believe a word. Funny though, I haven't heard much about you." The two of them laughed, making Wes blush.

"Shut up. Have you already played?" He indicated to Ash's spot on the other side of the window.

"No, just about to." Ash closed his journal and stood up. "Join me in a bit, show off your skills to Wyatt?" Cue another blush to Wes' cheeks.

"Yeah, maybe." Ash left them to it and made his way outside, almost body slamming Camille as she entered.

"Shit, sorry. You okay?" He asked, grabbing hold of her shoulders to stop her falling over.

"Yeah, I'm fine." She gently shook herself free from his hold, a hint of a blush on her sun-kissed skin.

Rubbing the back of his neck, Ash was beginning to feel a bit exposed to everyone watching. "Right, I'll let you go. I need to go and set up."

"Oh God, not more 90s alt rock tracks?" she groaned.

"And what's wrong with them?" he asked, a smile forming.

"They're so overdone by buskers. Why don't you try writing your own music rather than rely on covers of bands you can't ever hope to be better than."

Ouch.

"I have played one of my own songs from time to time. Maybe I will again if you promise to come and listen." Hope fluttered as she smiled at his words.

41

"Maybe I will. I'm not working and don't have anything better to do."

Double ouch. Ash watched as she walked away, swinging those hips, over to where Leah was behind the counter with a steaming cup waiting for her. Leah knew Ash wrote his own music and clearly hadn't mentioned it to Camille. Strangely, that hurt his feelings. He locked eyes with Leah, who made a waving motion with her hands, ushering him outside. Before he did, he went back over to his table.

"Wes, I need you, just for one song."

"Ash, I'm kinda busy here." Bro code for 'I'm on a date', but Ash didn't hear it.

"Please, just one. Just a quick performance of *Freedom for All*. I still have your cajon in my trunk. As soon as you're done, you can leave me alone and get back to this."

Wyatt was laughing watching the exchange.

"Go on, Wes. I want to see you in action."

"One song only." He stood up. Ash laughed and flung his arms around his ex-boyfriend.

"I owe you one."

"I intend to collect."

:: ::

Once he'd set up his mic stand, Ash ran back into the coffee house to grab a bottle of water, and to make sure Camille hadn't left. She hadn't. She was sat on a bar stool behind the counter, chatting to Leah who was working her way through a line of customers.

"You ready, music man?" Leah asked as she expertly mixed up a confusing as hell order as Ash put his money for his drink by the cash register.

"All set up. And I've had a request for something original too." He glanced at Camille who half smiled at him, confusion clear on her face.

"Make sure you prop that door open so we can hear."

Ash gave Leah a salute and left the store, making sure the door was wedged open. When he looked back, he could see the two girls having what looked like an intense conversation, as if Camille was finding out just how much Leah knew about him. The thought made him grin.

"You ready?" he asked Wes, who was sat on his cajon waiting for him.

"As I'll ever be. Remember, one song, no more. So, don't flash those big blue eyes at me

43

because after I put this back in your trunk, me and Wyatt are going down to the beach."

"Yes, boss."

Ash picked up his acoustic, plugged it into his amp and checked it was still tuned. Once he was ready, he gave Wes a nod and the drummer counted him in.

With a nod to each other they started the opening chords. By the time Ash had sung the first few lines they were smiling with satisfaction, as people began to come out of the coffee shop to watch them, Wyatt, Camille and Leah included. They worked the crowd, Ash making eye contact with different people.

When the song came to an end, Wyatt, Camille, and Leah whooped and started raucous applause. The crowd around them was bigger than it had ever been and the three of them were front row center. Ash grinned at everyone he made eye contact with, thanking them when they dropped money into his open guitar case. He'd not worn a beanie, so Wes had improvised.

"Right, we're going. Give me your keys so I can stow this." Wes hefted the cajon into his hands as Ash found his car keys.

"Don't forget to bring them back, I don't feel

like walking home." Wes nodded, before walking away with Wyatt.

"Well, music man, that was pretty good. I'll not admit to being impressed just yet, but damn, boy, you got some pipes." Leah patted his arm before going back to work. The crowd around him had started to disperse and soon there was only Camille left.

"What did you think? Can I give those 90s alt gods a run for their money?" he asked as he plucked a few strings on his guitar for something to do with his hands.

"Okay, you can write. And play. And sing. You got the whole package, don't you?"

"And that package would include...?" *Please say cute too.*

"Oh no! I'm not falling for that. You're good, let's leave it at that." She dropped a five-dollar bill into his case, smiled, and went back inside.

"Well, it's progress I guess," he muttered to himself as he began to play another song, a cover this time. Out of the corner of his eye, he could see Camille inside shaking her head at his choice of Panic! At the Disco's, *The Ballad of Mona Lisa.* "It's not 90s," he called out before he started to sing.

The open mic night was being held in a campus bar and when Rare Breed entered, it was packed to the rafters with people.

"Whoa, I think this is the most people we've ever played for," Joey commented as they fought their way through the crowd to find the organizer. To Ash's surprise, it was Leah.

"I was wondering when you'd show, music man." She grinned at him.

"Er, Ash. Who's this?" Chris asked, looking between Leah and his bandmate, grinning at her.

"Sorry, guys, Leah, this is Chris, Joey, and you've already met Wes. Guys, this is Leah who seems to be running the show tonight."

"Nice to meet you. I have you guys on last, so

make sure you give them something to remember. I gotta go, I'll catch you all later." With a flick of her long braids, Leah turned on her heel and moved away through the crowd. As they watched her move, he swore he heard Chris mumble 'she's hot' under his breath.

The guys managed to find a tiny, unsteady table to sit at. Joey had tried to buy them some beers but had been turned away with four bottles of soda. It had made him surly and was spoiling the vibe. In fact, the more Ash looked at him, he wondered if he'd already been drinking from his dad's stash before he got here. As they drank and watched the acts perform, Ash filled them in on how he knew Leah.

"So, is that the chick who inspired your song? Niiice." Joey asked checking her out as she stepped onto the small stage to announce the next performer, her short silver dress sparkling under the lights.

"No, that's Camille," Wes looked around the busy room. "Who I can't seem to see. Ow!" He rubbed his arm when Ash punched him.

"Who's Camille?" Chris asked, one eyebrow raised and a smile on his face.

"She's a cute barista in the coffee shop that Ash sings outside of," Wes told them.

"How would you know she's cute? She's not got a dick." Joey asked, not quite managing to hide the derision in his voice.

"I'm gay, not fucking blind," Wes snapped, shocking them all.

"Joey, bro. Stop being a little bitch to and about Wes. If this carries on, you'll have to leave the band, because it's just not acceptable," Ash spoke sternly, ready to hit the keyboard player.

Joey stood up, knocking his chair over. "You know what, screw this. I'm done. You always take his side over mine. Well fuck you. To be honest I've been talking to some other guys about a place in their band because you lot want to sing love songs and braid each other's hair. You've forgotten how to have fun. Good luck trying to find somewhere to rehearse after you come and get your shit tomorrow." He stormed out, no doubt toward the parking lot where his dad's van was parked.

"Did Joey just quit Rare Breed?" Chris asked, his pale cheeks flushed red.

"Yeah, I think so."

"Thank fuck for that." Chris picked up his

drink and took a long swig. "And I'm glad our stuff's in your car, Ash, otherwise we wouldn't be able to perform tonight." They'd decided on an acoustic show so they wouldn't have to bring all their gear for just one song. It had been another thing to piss Joey off. Him not being needed on keys meant he'd have had to pick up something like a tambourine which he said he found demeaning.

Ash could feel his hands shaking in rage. He was also glad Joey was gone. They'd all put up with his crappy attitude for too long, but to bail just before they were due to go up on stage. No, that was out of order.

Leah came over to their table. "Guys, you're up after the next act." Wait, where's the other guy?"

"He quit. Looks like we're a trio now."

"Well, you better get your trio asses backstage so you're ready to go on after Camille." Leah stalked away just as Camille walked on stage and sat behind a keyboard.

"What? *That's* Camille?" Chris asked. "She *is* cute." That comment earned him an elbow to the ribs from Wes as the two of them made their way backstage to grab their instruments. Ash couldn't move; he was entranced by Camille on stage singing.

"Bro, come on. We're on in a minute." Wes came back and grabbed him by his jacket as Camille's song came to an end. Running through the thinning crowd, the guys were ready just in time. As Ash passed Camille on her way from the stage, he grinned at her.

"Yeah, okay. I get it now," he said before emerging on stage, his acoustic in his hand to join the others. Wes sat on his cajon while Chris's acoustic bass was slung over his shoulder as they both waited for him.

"Hey, we're Rare Breed, and this is *Lost in Translation*."

:: ::

Usually after a show, the guys would pile into the garage at Joey's to deconstruct their performance and find ways to improve – 'nit-picking by Ash' as Wes usually called it. They'd teased him for years about being a perfectionist; he preferred to call himself driven, but they never listened. On this night, the three of them climbed into Ash's car and he drove them to his house where they piled into his bedroom.

When they'd come off stage, he'd looked for Camille, but couldn't find her, so he had no choice but to leave without saying goodbye.

"Did you see the reaction we got tonight?" Chris was still on a high and was bouncing around Ash's room like a lanky five-year old on a sugar high.

"Students love us it would seem. We should book more student nights." Wes looked up from his phone, which had been in his hand from the moment they'd got into the car. "Why haven't we done any before?"

"Yeah, Ash. Why haven't we done student venues before?" Chris asked as Wes pulled him to sit down in the hopes he'd calm down.

"We need to be where agents and managers are. That's the way we'll get noticed."

"Yeah, but we need fans to fill venues."

Ash thought about Wes' words and realized he wasn't wrong.

"I mean, we have the social media accounts and we hardly have any followers apart from girls who like Ash's arms and think Chris is adorable. Yeah, they enjoy the music, but it's not the same.

We need followers who are in it for the music alone. Also, we need to address the fact that Joey quit on us." Wes was always the one who seemed to have his head screwed on. Ash was all about making it big while Chris was simply loving life.

"Ah, Joseph. What are we going to do about him?" Chris asked.

"What can we do? He's a dick for what he said about Wes, and for quitting. We can't force him to be in the band, and if I'm honest, I don't want a bigot playing with us," Ash snapped, instantly regretting it. "Sorry bro, I'm not pissed at you."

"I know. I also know that Joey doesn't know you're not straight like him and me, so I get why you're pissed. You're right, he's a bigot, but a, where are we going to rehearse, and b, he was our keyboard player. No offence, bro, you're good on a piano, but he's better."

Ash couldn't disagree. For all his faults, Joey was an epic pianist whereas he could tinker when he was writing a song.

"Yet look at how great we sounded tonight without him. And the reaction we got."

"That's a point. Anyhow, it's too late to make any decisions now. We can do that once we collect our gear from the studio tomorrow. D'you think your dad will loan us the station wagon for Wes' drums? Shit, where the hell are we gonna store it all?" Chris was starting to spiral. It was usually Wes, but he was still distracted by his phone. Judging by the small smile on his face, Ash guessed he was texting with Wyatt, and that pleased him. His friend deserved to be happy.

"Something else we need to deal with tomorrow. Let's get some sleep, boys." He flicked off his lamp as the three of them settled in to share his bed, something they always did when the three of them were together.

Squashed between his two best friends, Ash couldn't sleep. All he could think about was how good Camille had been up on stage. He knew she was studying music, but for some reason, the idea of her being a performer never even crossed his mind.

Careful not to wake Chris or Wes, he shimmied himself out of bed, and grabbed his journal and phone before making his way down to the den. He curled up on the end of the couch and flicked through the pages of his journal, making a mental note to get a new one as it was almost full.

"You okay, son?" His dad's voice was quiet in

the dim light as the older Kane reached the bottom of the stairs.

"Yeah, couldn't sleep. Too much of a buzz still."

"How did it go?"

His dad sat down as Ash began to fill him in. When he got to the part about Joey being a dick and quitting, his dad snorted.

"What?"

"I always knew there was something off about that kid."

"Really?" Ash was shocked. He knew his parents adored Wes and Chris and had assumed they felt the same about the third of their quartet.

"Yeah. He never seemed to join in, was always on the periphery whenever you boys were here. And to find out his... opinions, for want of a better word about Wes... well, that's completely unacceptable."

"Yeah, but it's left us stranded."

"We'll work that all out together."

For the first time in a long time, Ash hugged his dad.

"I really got lucky in the parent department," he mumbled into his dad's shoulder.

7

Mr. Kane insisted on borrowing a neighbor's trailer that he hitched on the back of his car, then he drove them over to Joey's place to pick up their gear. Chris had already sent a text to warn him, and when they pulled up, he was waiting for them by the side gate.

"Hey," he greeted them, not making eye contact with any of them. His face dropped a little when he saw Ash's dad had come with them. "Hi, Mr. Kane."

"Hi, Joey." Neither of them said any more as Ash, his dad, Chris, and Wes made their way into the garage to start clearing out their stuff while Joey watched from outside the doors. It took them an hour to gather instruments and other music equipment which Ash's dad made sure was loaded carefully in the trailer while the guys made sure they hadn't left anything else. Eventually, the studio they'd rehearsed in for over three years looked empty, making Ash realize it was him, Wes, and Chris who filled the room. All Joey had was a couple of his guitars, and a couple of old garden chairs. The rest was loaded up ready to be stored somewhere until they found somewhere new, even the flea market couch had been piled into the trailer.

"It didn't need to be like this, Joe," Ash told his friend, or was that ex-friend? "It really didn't."

"I think it did. Not because of Wes and his... well, you know."

Ash grit his teeth to stop him from punching Joey.

"Because I'm going to college in the fall. Out of state."

"Dude, that's amazing. You could have told us; you know that, don't you?" Joey nodded. "Is that the only reason you quit Rare Breed?" He needed to know if the bigotry was an act and excuse to leave the band, or if it was how Joey really felt.

"Not the only reason. I shouldn't have said you always take Wes' side, but I just can't..."

"Can't what? Be in a band with a gay guy?" Anger began to fill Ash and he clenched his fist at his side.

"I'm sorry. I know it's wrong, but I just can't."

Suddenly, Ash's rage at Joey exploded and words began tumbling out of his mouth. He didn't even care if they were coherent or not, they just needed to be said.

"Well, it's lucky you fucking quit then. Wouldn't want to be associated with a gay guy, or a bi one for that matter. You're a douche, Joey Wilson, a grade A douche and I'm just sorry we wasted three fucking years on you."

Ash stalked away before he hit his old friend.

"Wait, who's bi?" Joey called out.

"Me, you prick. Oh, and I dated Wes. I hid it from you because you're a complete prick, Joey. You're also a disgusting bigot and I hope you fester in it." Slamming the gate closed behind him was the only satisfaction he got from the entire encounter.

"Everything okay?" his dad asked when he reached the car.

"No, but it will be now the trash has taken itself out." Chris and Wes crowded Ash and his dad, their hands automatically grabbing hold of him to ground and calm him down.

"You know, I'm proud of you boys. None of you have the easiest lives to live, but you live them with your heads held high. Now, let's go."

The three friends climbed into the back seat to maintain the comfort of their physical contact as Ash's dad drove them away from Joey's house. None of them turned to look behind them, none of them saw him watching them from the gate.

:: ::

It had been a week since the blowout with Joey, and the three of them felt that the band was already better off without him. They'd spent the majority of their time reworking their songs for three rather than the original quartet. They'd dropped the few songs Joey had written from their set. Their gear was still in storage and Wes was missing his drum kit as they scouted for rehearsal space they could afford. While Ash's parents were being cool lately about the band, they had insisted that the guys support themselves. If they wanted to make it, seriously make it, in the music business, they wanted all three of them to be aware of everything and to be able to support themselves.

While Wes and Chris were at school, Ash sat in the coffee shop as he scoured the classified ads but couldn't find anything. He was getting frustrated and it was affecting his ability to write.

"Yo, music man, 'sup?" Leah called out as he walked into the shop after playing outside for three hours.

"Hey, Leah." He dropped his backpack at his feet as he waited at the counter for his coffee. "Wait, 'yo? Really?"

She merely grinned at him as he shuffled his feet against the vinyl flooring beneath his sneakers.

"Whoa, you look down. Want a muffin?"

"No, thanks anyway." He paid for his drink, leaving her a tip, and made his way over to his regular table. Minutes later, Leah placed a muffin in front of him.

"It's on me. You look like you need it, and to

talk." She sat down. Ash looked over her shoulder to see Brian standing behind the counter serving.

"It's fine, Leah. You have to work." He broke off a piece of the muffin and put it in his mouth. "Oh, man, this is amazing."

"Thanks." The smug look on her face made him smile.

"You made this?" He was impressed. "Girl, there's no end to your talents." Leah nodded her head, accepting the compliment.

"You best believe it, now talk."

After a moment, Ash let the entire story out. Everything about Joey, his and Wes' past, and the struggle to find a rehearsal space.

"I can't help with Joey, but it sounds like you got out of a mess there. No one needs a so-called friend bringing them down, not letting them be their true selves. But the rehearsal space I might be able to help you with."

"Really? That would be epic if you could."

"Leave it with me. Give me your number so I can scope it out and get back to you." Even before she finished speaking, he'd ripped out a page from his journal and scribbled his number on it. Leah's face screwed up when she read it. "Uh, is this a seven? What about this? I *think* it's a four."

Rolling his eyes, he handed her his pen and rattled off his cell number. Someone else to give him crap about his handwriting.

"Thanks for this, Leah, seriously."

"It might take me a couple of days to get it sorted, but as soon as I know, you will." She stood up and looked down at him. "I need to get back to work, but don't ever let anyone dull your shine."

"I won't." He grinned up at her before she turned and made her way back to work.

:: ::

It took Leah three days to text him. He was packing up after a not-so-stellar performance outside *Downtown Beans*.

Meet me at this address at 4. I want to show you something.

A fizzle of excitement flowed through Ash as he read the message. He hadn't told Chris or Wes about the potential new rehearsal space yet because he didn't want to get their hopes up.

I'll be there.

After putting his phone back in his pocket, he

packed his stuff away, climbed into his car, and went home.

The house was quiet as both his parents were still at work, so he went straight up to his bedroom and lay down on his bed for a while. Almost every day since the blow out with Joey, whenever he slowed down enough, his mind travelled to hearing Camille sing on stage at the open mic night. Her voice was incredible, and he couldn't get the song she'd sung out of his head. He hadn't seen her since as she was busy working on a composition for college – so Leah had told him – and it was killing him not being able to talk to her about her music. Frustration ranged through him as he pulled himself to his feet and went back outside, ready to go and meet Leah. As he walked along the drive to his car, his mom pulled up in her own car.

"You off out, love?"

"Yeah, got a lead on a rehearsal space to check out."

"That's great, will you be home for dinner?"

"Hopefully." He kissed her on the cheek and unlocked his car. He could see his mom in his mirrors, watching him from the drive as he peeled away along the street.

"You found it okay?" Leah stated the obvious as he climbed out of his car. When he simply raised an eyebrow at her, she rolled her eyes and led him through a gate that led into a garden that was full of overgrown trees and bushes.

"What is this place?"

"Just follow me." She was being coy, and he couldn't understand why. The garage she led him to looked almost identical to the one in Joey's back yard, just in much better condition. It had clearly been well maintained and a weird feeling washed over him. Coughing to cover his awkwardness, he came to a stop behind Leah. "It needs a bit of work, but it's soundproof and would fit all your gear inside."

With a flourish, she slid open the doors and gestured for him to enter. The space was amazing but smelled musty and unused. It was in need of a bit of redecoration to cover the peeling paint. It had a very similar layout to their old studio but Ash noted where it was different. There was still a loft area, but a metal spiral staircase led up to it rather than a rickety wooden one and the loft area looked much sturdier judging by the pile of boxes stored up there. Standing in the middle of the empty space, he turned in a circle taking everything in.

"This place is gnarly. I don't think we'll be able afford it." It killed him to say it, but he needed to be clear on the band's budget, or lack of.

"That's the thing. All Mr. Rogers wants is a hundred dollars so he can clean it out and repaint it. After that, it's rent free for as long as you need it."

"Who's Mr. Rogers?"

"Camille's dad."

8

W es and Chris stared at him as if he'd sprouted wings.

"Camille, as in the girl you're crushing on. We're renting rehearsal space from her dad?"

"I'm not crushing on her," Ash lied, ignoring the pointed looks from his two best friends. "But that's beside the point. The space is amazing, better than Joey's garage. And Mr. Rogers repainted it and the soundproofing's top spec. We'll be able to jam as loud as we like without getting noise complaints."

"I'm not sure about this..." Wes trailed off. Ash knew the drummer would cave. He just needed to get Chris on side.

"Just come and take a look with me. Mr.

Rogers has said we can do whatever we want with the space and we'll even be the only ones with a key so we can keep our gear safe. Let me take you over there now so you can at least check it out." Ash's foot tapped with his eagerness.

"We'll look, but no promises." Chris pointed a finger at him, wagging it the way Ash's mom used to when they were kids in elementary school getting caught eating cookies before dinner.

With a grin, Ash led them out to his car and drove over to Camille's dad's house. He still couldn't get his head around the fact that it was Camille's dad's place. Leah had arranged for them to use a space where Camille grew up. He hardly knew the girl, and as much as he couldn't stop thinking about her, he was trying to ignore how weird this arrangement had the potential to be.

"Does she know about this?" Wes asked as Ash drove.

"Who? Camille? Apparently, Leah okayed it with her before going to speak to her dad about it."

"And she's okay with it?"

"So, Leah said. Look, I haven't seen her to ask

her permission, but if her best friend says it cool, then it must be cool." Ash pulled up outside the house and led the guys through the side gate and over to the garage.

"Woah, déjà vu much?" Chris could see the similarities to Joey's place too.

"Yeah, I know. But we need a space. Come inside, then make up your minds." He slid the doors open and gestured for them to enter.

"Man, you're right. It's perfect." Wes stood in the center of the room, turning in slow circles to take the whole place in, just as Ash had done.

"Right? There's even a bathroom with a shower out the back, which means we wouldn't be disturbing Mr. Rogers every time Chris drinks too much soda and needs to go to the bathroom every five minutes." Ash and Wes laughed at the face Chris pulled. "We could put the couch on this wall, your drums over here, and we'd still have a bunch of space."

Ash couldn't contain the excitement that was brimming over as he bounced on the balls of his feet, watching as his bandmates wandered around the large, empty room.

"And it's really free?" Wes asked, still not believing their good luck.

"Well, after we reimburse Mr. Rogers for decorating and stuff, yeah."

"When can we move our stuff in?" Chris asked, a wide grin on his flushed face.

"Whenever you boys like." A man's voice made them jump. They whirled around to face the doors, where Mr. Rogers stood, leaning up against the frame.

:: ::

The following day, Ash's dad borrowed the trailer again, and he and the guys loaded all their gear up from the storage unit and took it over to Camille's dad's place, ready to get their studio set up. When they arrived, Ash insisted his dad go and get to know Mr. Rogers while he, Wes, and Chris sorted the space out how they wanted it.

"Bro, I still can't believe you found us this sweet rehearsal space." Chris grinned as he and Ash carried the couch through the double doors while Wes set up his drum kit.

"Dude, it was all Leah. We owe that girl huge."

"Maybe we can buy her something to say thanks?" Wes suggested. Ash nodded in agreement but had no idea what. He barely knew Leah; even less than he knew Camille.

"So... does Camille spend much time here?" Wes asked him slyly as Ash collapsed onto the couch, relishing in its well-worn comfort.

"I doubt it. She lives in dorms with Leah, which is why the space is free. Apparently, her mom used to use it as an art studio and her dad had it soundproofed because she used to blare music really loudly while she painted, and while Camille practiced her scales and shit. Or so Leah said."

"Her mom is artistic? Cool. I'd like to meet her."

"Yeah, well. You can't." Ash and his friends whirled around to see a kid who looked to be around thirteen standing in the door. "And please, don't mention my mom to my sister."

"Oh, hey. Er... why can't we meet her?" Chris asked, clearly not reading the atmosphere in the room.

"Because she left us almost two years ago. It crushed us all when she decided she'd had enough of being a Rogers and moved across town, but my sister took it the hardest. She stopped playing piano and almost didn't go to college.

Camille only picked up a guitar because she could never completely give up music because it's pretty much *who* she is, but she wanted to cut off ties with Mom."

Ash's heart clenched at the kid's words. He could hear the pain in them, but the kid had tried to be as matter of fact as he could.

"Did your mom play?" Wes asked, softly.

"God no. She was an elementary teacher and artist, and she was a huge music fan, but couldn't sing a note to save her life, but when Camille turned out to be some music prodigy, they, we, used to spend so much time out here listening to records and having these great dance parties and my sister used to practice out here. So yeah, don't mention Mom to her. It's hard for her to come out here, which is why it's so empty and unused."

"We promise." Ash approached Camille's brother, his hand held out. "I'm Ash. This is Wes and big mouth over there is Chris."

"I'm Ben." He entered the garage and looked around. The walls were bare, and their instruments weren't set up properly, but he still nodded his head in approval. "It's gonna look pretty sick in here when you're all set up."

"Cheers, little dude. Do you play?" Chris asked him.

"Not really, I always wanted to learn, but by the time I realized just how much, Camille was at college and didn't have the time so I never mentioned it."

"What instrument?"

"I always wanted to be able to shred on the guitar."

"Hey, Ash can teach you. He's a great teacher." Wes called out from behind his growing drum kit. Ash managed to hold in the groan that almost escaped him when Ben's face lit up.

"Yeah? Oh my God, that would be *awesome.* I know you guys are gonna be busy, so I won't get in the way, but I would love that."

"Hey, hold on a second." Ash ran out to his dad's car where there were still a few boxes. Finding the one he was looking for, he carried it into the garage. "Here, take these. Do you have a guitar of your own?"

"No, I never got round to buying one. After she left and Camille went to college, it didn't seem important."

"I'll bring my junior acoustic over for you when we're all ready to start. These are the beginner books my mom and dad got me when I was a kid."

"Seriously? You're letting me borrow these?"

"Little dude, you can have them. I don't need them anymore. But the guitar will be a loan. It was my first one, and..."

"That's awesome, thanks, man. Is it okay if I go and show these to my dad?"

"Crack on, kid." With a sloppy fist bump, Ben ran out of the garage, a huge grin on his face.

"You know, I never realized you're actually a nice guy." Chris commented, earning him a slap to the chest from Ash. "But seriously, I think you just made little dude's year."

Unsure what to think or how to react, Ash coughed before helping Wes with setting up the drums.

:: ::

"Tell me about your new studio." Ash's mom said as the three of them sat around the small kitchen table eating dinner.

"Oh, Mom, it's so cool. Mr. Rogers had it all soundproofed a few years ago, so we don't have to control our volume." Ash ran off on a tangent telling her about the garage. Both of his parents watched his enthusiasm with smiles on their faces, but he noticed his mom's was tinged with a bit of sadness. Her disappointment in him had never really gone away, despite the truce they seemed to be having recently. She'd calmed down ever since he turned eighteen just before finishing his senior year at school.

"And this Mr. Rogers, is he okay?" This question she aimed at her husband.

"He passed the test, honey. He's a thoroughly lovely man. He has two kids, a daughter around Ash's age and a younger son. He's a realtor and after his wife left him, the family didn't need to use the space any longer." At his mom's confused face, Ash's dad went on to explain about Camille's mom's love for music and the horrible way she'd upped and abandoned her young family. Not wanting to overhear anything he shouldn't, Ash excused himself and went up to his room.

He couldn't wait to let himself into their new studio space to work on some writing after he finished up outside the coffee shop. He also wondered when Camille would be back at work.

9

S etting up his mic stand outside the coffee house; Ash couldn't help but notice Camille wasn't inside and felt a wave of disappointment wash over him once more. As soon as he was set up, and his guitar case was open at his feet, he started to play the legendary opening riff to Guns 'n' Roses' *Sweet Child O' Mine*. It wasn't a song he performed much, but it was a jam and for some reason he'd woken up with it in his head that morning.

"At least it's not alt. But really, could you be any more of a busking cliché?"

Ash smiled at the sound of Camille's voice as he sang, causing a couple of people walking past to sing along with the chorus which only made her roll her eyes at the smug smile he knew was on his face.

He noticed she hung around until he finished singing, watching people interact with him and when he'd finished the song, he turned to her, finding her watching him.

"What?" He rubbed at his face, worried he had something on it.

"Oh, nothing." There was that hint of a blush again. He was growing more than a little fond of the flush of pink to her naturally tan skin. He often pictured it when he thought of her, not missing the fact it had a certain effect on him when he did think about it. Coughing to alter his train of thought, he forced himself to make eye contact with her.

"Well, you seem very interested in 'nothing' standing there."

Another eyeroll which made him laugh.

"I like watching musicians perform. Especially ones who know how to work a crowd."

"Wait, was that a compliment, Ms. Rogers?" His use of her surname seemed to shock her.

"How did you kno- oh, yeah. Dad." Once again, he laughed. "How are you finding the garage?"

"Oh, it's great. Why don't you use it? You're a phenomenal performer yourself." Ash wasn't above giving a pretty girl a compliment, especially one who was so crazy talented the way Camille was.

"It was a space I shared with my mom and the rest of my family, but that all changed. And I'm not a performer, I'm a songwriter." He was confused.

"Aren't they the same thing?"

"Not really. I write songs, I just don't like singing them, you know like Piper Perabo in *Coyote Ugly?* Just without the crippling stage fright."

Ash couldn't imagine not singing his own songs, especially ones that were personal to him. The idea of handing them over to another artist to do whatever they wanted with them made him break out into a cold sweat.

"Well, I think it's a waste of your voice."

"You sound like Leah." Camille laughed. "I've never wanted the limelight the way most musicians do. I don't want to be center stage, all eyes on me. I'm perfectly content being a purely background player."

"I gotta admit, I don't get it, but I guess everyone needs to have a dream."

Silence fell over them and to prevent any awkwardness, he strummed a few chords on his guitar.

"That's nice. Is it one of yours?"

"Yeah, just something I'm trying to work out." He could see Brian watching them from inside. By the look on his face, he wasn't impressed Camille was talking to him so much.

"Hey, your boyfriend's watching us."

Camille followed his line of vision. "Huh? Oh, that's Brian. He's the assistant manager, and, oh shoot, I'm late for my shift. I gotta run."

"Oh, before you go. Any requests?"

"Yeah, something from this century." She slipped into the coffee house laughing at him.

Immediately, Ash began to play a song he would never normally be caught singing in public. One Direction's *No Control*. It wasn't a song he should know, but thanks to Lizzie playing their albums constantly, it was one that had got stuck in his head. Even more so when she told him that she'd read rumors online that it was a song about waking up with morning wood. As he sang, he looked through the window to see

Camille laughing at him which only made him smile wider.

He didn't miss the glare he received from Brian though.

:: ::

"Hey, dude. You need to check this out," Chris called out to him the minute he walked into the new studio, which was starting to look like their own space thanks to the posters and pictures they'd stuck to the walls.

"What's got your panties in a bunch, Christian?" he asked, laughing at the screwed-up face Chris pulled as he angled the laptop in front of him to face Ash. It was open on a YouTube page. As he sat down, his friend pressed play.

"Wait... is that... us?" Ash watched the video. It had clearly been recorded on a phone at the open mic night, but the sound quality was brilliant, and, even if he did say so himself, they sounded amazing. It had been a one song performance, but the crowd had loved it.

"Yeah, it was posted yesterday, and check out the views it's got. Almost a hundred thousand. Bro, this is epic."

As a band, they'd posted videos online before, but no one had seemed to take any notice. This was different. This was someone in the audience. This was showing them at their best with an audience loving what they were doing.

"We're Rare Breed, check us out." Chris' voice sounded through the laptop speakers as the video came to an end.

"This is insane." Ash could feel himself practically vibrating at the idea of so many people having watched a video of them performing live. "Oh, what do the comments say?"

Well, the majority of them are about your muscly arms." Wes nudged him, laughing. Ash always wore sleeveless shirts on stage – most of the time in fact – as he claimed it helped him move around easier and helped prevent him overheating on stage.

"Any comments about the actual music, Wesley?"

"Yes, *Ashley,* people love the track."

"We totally need to ride this. Like post more videos online. Maybe we can record some rehearsals and stuff like that."

"What about your hordes of female fans?" Chris was laughing at Ash having female fans swooning over his arms. "Maybe a few videos of you lifting weights would draw them in."

"Fuck off," he snapped, instantly feeling guilty at the flush of red on Chris' pale face that blended in with his bright hair. He didn't do well with people arguing at the best of times, even more so when it was aimed at him.

Chris raised his hands. "Okay, chill, bro. I was joking."

"Sorry, Chris, I just want the music to speak to people, not the fact I show some skin at shows." Ash sighed.

"Well, you got the good genes. You can't help being the good looking one." Ash rolled his eyes. "And if it brings the fans in staring at you, then they can see you're not just a pretty boy when they hear you, right?"

"Oh shut up," Ash shook his head at Chris in mock protest of his comments, "and let's get some work done. Oh, has Ben been down, I brought my junior for him?"

"Wow, I honestly thought you'd forget that. No, he hasn't been down."

"I'll run it over to the house, and then we can get started."

Ash left his friends watching the video again

and walked over to the house, a small guitar case in his hand. Mr. Rogers had told them if they ever needed anything, they could knock on the kitchen door as that was where he and Ben spent most of their time. Shuffling his feet a little, Ash knocked and within minutes, he was face-to-face with Camille.

10

"Uhm, hi. I was looking for Ben."

"Oh, sure. Come in, I'll call him down for you." Camille stepped to one side to let Ash into the kitchen. As he passed her, he could smell coffee on her hair, which she was wearing loose, the curls framing her face. After she closed the door, she walked across the room to the bottom of the stairs and called out her brother's name. Within seconds, the sound of feet thundering down the wooden stairs filled the air.

"Oh, hey, Ash." The younger Rogers grinned at him while Camille watched them with a small smile on her face.

"Here you go, little dude. As promised."

"Oh my god, I honestly thought you'd forget."

"Why does everyone keep saying that to me?"

Camille snorted as she turned away, her shoulders shaking. He guessed she was laughing at him.

"Thanks Ash, this is awesome. I'll start practicing once I've done my homework." Without saying anything else, Ben ran back upstairs, sounding like a herd of baby elephants on the stairs.

"What was that about?" Camille asked him as she sat on one of the stools at the island.

"Ben asked for guitar lessons, so I loaned him my junior acoustic and gave him some beginner books."

"I didn't know he wanted to learn." Her voice was soft as she looked away from him and suddenly, Ash wasn't sure what to say. He didn't know how much she'd want to talk about her mom with a stranger.

"Yeah, he said he wanted lessons, but then... other things got in the way." *Not the best way to phrase it there, bro.*

"Oh. Right. And you're going to give him lessons?"

"Sure, why not?"

"That's... that's really sweet of you, thanks." Ash basked in the second compliment from Camille in one day.

"It's cool." He shrugged, trying to play it all down.

"You do realize that my dad will probably try and pay you."

"And I'll refuse. He's letting us use the garage for nothing, so the least I could do is give Ben a couple of guitar lessons a week."

"You clearly don't know my dad." Camille smiled as the man himself walked into the room.

"Don't know what about me?" He looked at the two of them, confusion written all over his face. Camille quickly filled him in about Ash teaching her brother to play the guitar.

"And she's right, you should be paid for your time."

"No, Mr. Rogers. I can't take your money. We're already taking up space in your garage."

"Don't be ridiculous, Ash. That's different. That's for your band to rehearse so you can make it. This is you taking time out of your day to teach my son a skill. I'll research the going rates for music tutors and will pay you. No arguments."

Ash was struck dumb. How the hell did he get so lucky recently?

"Nod your head and agree. It's the only way," Camille told him. He did as he was told.

"Oh, I saw the video of you guys earlier," Mr. Rogers told Ash. "You guys are good, better than I expected if I'm honest." No doubt he'd been picturing some grungy garage band that were often shown in the movies, and Ash couldn't help but grin at the idea.

"What video?" Camille asked, confused. Mr. Rogers made to grab at his laptop to, Ash assumed, show his daughter the video of them at the open mic night.

"I er... I best get back to the guys." Feeling a bit embarrassed, Ash made his escape out of the kitchen and back into the garage where he instantly felt at ease.

"You look like you've seen a ghost," Chris told him as he collapsed onto the couch.

"Nah, just a bit overwhelmed." To distract himself, he pulled his journal out of his backpack. "Right, let's get to work."

:: ::

For four hours, Rare Breed jammed out the hardest they had in a while. Having a space where they could completely let go made all the difference, and knowing this space was sound-proofed added a little extra something, or so Ash thought at least.

Sweat was dripping off him as he pulled his shirt off to wipe at the back of his neck.

"Boys, we are *on fire*. I need to scout out some gigs because this new vibe is being wasted on this garage." The others nodded as Ash walked out to the small bathroom at the back of the garage and splashed some cold water from the hand basin onto his face and the back of his neck. As he looked in the mirror above it, he could see how alive he looked. His face was flushed, his eyes were bright, and he could feel it deep within himself. This was going to be Rare Breed's time. It *needed* to be. He made a mental note to check his usual haunts to find out if there were any openings for him and his boys to play.

Air drying his still clammy skin off due to the lack of towels in their small bathroom, he walked out into their studio to start again after grabbing a fresh shirt from his backpack. He rubbed the old and damp one over his hair in an attempt to rid it of the sweat as much as he could. It wasn't helping.

"Boys, I really think we're gonna do it this time, gonna get the notice we've worke- Oh, hey." Camille was standing in the center of the garage, staring at him. Distantly, he could hear Chris sniggering.

"Uhm, hi. I... er... I..." She coughed to clear her throat before trying again. "Could you put a shirt on, please?"

Wes barked out a laugh, startling Ash who had almost forgotten his friends were still in the same room. As he walked over to his backpack that rested on the couch, he realized what was wrong with Camille. Standing up, with a clean shirt in his hand, he turned to face her again. Out of the corner of his eye, he could see Wes shooting him a death glare.

"So, did you need something?" he asked, making sure to take his sweet time putting the shirt on, stretching as he did so. He noticed Camille wasn't looking directly at him and that made him smirk to himself.

"Nothing in particular." Once his shirt was

covering him, even his arms this time, she looked at him, the blush on her face deeper than he'd seen it before. "I just thought I'd come and check you guys out after Dad showed me that video."

"Sweet, you saw our video. What did you think? We were awesome, right?" Chris bounced over to her, his lanky form almost toppling over in his haste. "I'm Chris by the way. It's nice to meet you." The closer he got to her, Camille took a step backward, making Ash smile. Chris wasn't the best at personal space boundaries.

"Jeez, dude, give the girl some space and stop bombarding her with questions." He turned back to face Camille. "Sorry about him, he's like a big, ginger puppy sometimes."

"It's fine." She held out a hand for Chris to shake. "The video was so good. It made me sorry I had to leave straight after I finished up. I would have loved to have heard you perform live."

"In that case, take a seat and you can hear it now." Chris led her over to the couch and gently pushed her down into it. "Come on, boys, we have an audience. Plus, *Lost in Translation* sounds better on the electric over acoustic. Come on, Ash, get yourself ready."

Whenever Chris got like this, Ash found it was best to just go with it, so he did what he was told and moved back over to the guys and picked up his guitar.

"One, two, three."

11

After locking up the garage and pocketing his key, Ash led Wes and Chris over to his car, which Mr. Rogers let them park on his drive. Ash had tried to argue against it, but as he was the only one in the house who had a car, he insisted there was plenty of space.

"Chris, where are you tonight?" Ash asked as he reversed out and pulled away from the house.

"I'm at home." He didn't sound pleased about it, but he'd told them his parents were going through a rare good patch, so he wanted to spend as much time in his own space while it lasted.

"No worries, bro." Ash headed in the direction of Chris' house. Wes would be staying at his again. His mom had offered to make up the spare room for Wes as he was spending more time at their house than his own, but he'd refused. Ash knew it was because of his sister. Lizzie was sixteen and the two of them were close as hell, and Wes didn't want to leave her at home to deal with everything. But, because she was straight, did well at school, and wanted to go to college, she was safe. The two of them saw one another at school all the time, and she even came over to watch them rehearse now and then. He made a mental note to invite her to their new rehearsal space as soon as possible.

Once Ash's mom had fed the two of them and handed them piles of clean laundry, they went up to his room. As they settled down, Wes catching up with some homework and himself with his journal, a thought occurred to him. It wasn't a new one, but it crept up on him now and again. The fact the two of them had been a couple for a while should have caused a certain amount of awkwardness between them, but coming to the agreement it wasn't working had only made them stronger. Although he'd known Wes, Chris, and Joey for the same length of time, Wes had always been his closest friend. Neither of them could pinpoint why, it was just how it was. It didn't mean either of them liked Chris or Joey any less, in fact they adored the bones of Chris. Joey... well, he'd always been a bit pricklier.

Joey had always taken some sort of offence to how close the two of them were, even without knowing about them being a thing, but to Chris it had never been an issue. The third of their now trio was the easiest going of them all and was just happy to have friends who didn't judge him when he climbed through their bedroom windows at crazy hours of the night.

Apart from their shared love of music, the four friends had started Rare Breed as an escape. Now, without Joey, they needed it more than ever, especially Wes and Chris. Ash knew he was the lucky one of them all, with his stable home life. Even his arguments with his parents were seen as normal for an eighteen-year-old, as they accepted him and his life choices most of the time, even if they weren't happy with them.

"Ten bucks says two am this time," Wes muttered as he made himself comfortable on the airbed.

"You're on." They both knew things at Chris' house could change in a nanosecond and would.

"So, Camille?" Wes spoke without looking at Ash as he scrolled through his phone.

"What about her?" He managed to hide the smile that sprang to his face at the mere mention of her name as he scolded himself for being so obvious.

"Dude, you tormented her this afternoon."

"How did I? She's the one who appeared out of nowhere."

"Ashley Kane, we are using her dad's garage as a rehearsal space, for free I might add; of course she's going to be around. You didn't have to put on a show and embarrass her."

"It was just a bit of fun, but I promise to behave if she comes in again."

"You better. It's clear she likes you and you flaunting the goods that you claim shouldn't be a draw for fans of the band isn't going to get you anywhere with her."

As always, Wes was right.

"I'm sorry."

"You don't need to apologize to me. I enjoyed the view just as much as she did, but I'm also used to it." Ash barked out a laugh.

"Oh, speaking of views. When is Wyatt gonna come and watch us rehearse?" Before

Wes could reply, there was a knock on the window. Seeing it wasn't even one am, he slapped ten dollars into Ash's hand and went to let Chris in.

:: ::

Ash pulled into the parking lot at the school to pick up Chris and Wes. As usual, he was early, so he climbed out of the car and sat on the hood with his journal and lost himself in the words he was scribbling on the pages in front of him. Ever since Wes had pulled him up for teasing Camille, he hadn't been able to get her out of his head. Her long, curly hair that had smelled like coffee in her dad's kitchen, the small smile she'd had when she watched him with her brother, and the blush that was fucking adorable and made his body react the way only an eighteen-year-old's could.

Looking around the school he'd attended for four years, the place Rare Breed was born, he couldn't picture himself wandering the halls. He'd never been hugely popular; he and the boys had been seen as outcasts which hadn't bothered them at all. It gave them more freedom to find somewhere to rehearse their music, or for Ash to hide away with his journal.

He wondered what kind of friends Camille had hung around with at school. He imagined she and Leah walked to the beats of their own drums, not falling in with the cliques, and the thought made him smile as the lot around him filled up with students who had been let out.

A petite brunette approached him with a smile.

"You're Ashley Kane, right?" She asked, standing next to her car, which was parked up next to Ash's Chevy.

"Yeah." Feeling uncomfortable, he closed his journal and crossed his legs rather than have them stretched out in front of him.

"I'm Nikita. I saw the video of your band on YouTube and thought you guys were awesome."

"Thanks, that's great to hear."

"I was wondering... if you have a girlfriend."

"Er... no, no I don't." He answered automatically, even though it had nothing to do with her.

"Oh, that's grea- I mean, I'm surprised." She giggled and flicked her hair over her shoulder. "A great looking guy like you being single."

"Oh, I never said I was single. I just said I

didn't have a girlfriend." He knew he shouldn't have teased her, but he didn't know her, and she was getting way too personal.

"You're gay?" She spluttered out before turning away to unlock her car. Ash swore he heard her muttering to herself and it sounded like 'typical' to him, making him laugh to himself.

As she pulled out of her space, he spotted Joey across the lot watching him. Unsure what to do, Ash raised his hand in a half wave. His former bandmate nodded his head in acknowledgment before getting into a car that wasn't Ash's, which was weird after him riding with them for so long.

"Hey, bro, what you been up to today?" Chris appeared next to the car, dropping his backpack on the hood next to Ash's knee. It took a while for Ash to respond as he watched the car Joey was in drive away.

:: ::

As the rain began, Ash finished up the song he was singing and began to pack his gear away. It had been a quiet day outside the coffee house, and he hadn't made much money. While frustrating, he tried to not let it annoy him. It was a risk he took by busking, and one his parents reminded him of often. This was, they said, why he should get himself a proper, legal job to earn enough money for him to put back into the band. He was beginning to wonder if they were right.

After loading up the trunk of his car, he decided to go and spend some of his earnings in the coffee house. It was still early, and he was on his own. Wes and Wyatt were off doing God only knew what, but as Lizzie was with them, he knew it wouldn't be too X-rated. He didn't know where Chris was, he hadn't heard from him all day. As he waited to be served by Camille, he fired off a text checking if his bassist was okay.

"Hey, Ash, your usual?" Camille asked him, a wide smile on her face, which made the breath catch in his throat for a second.

"Yeah, sure. Thanks."

"Go and sit down, I'll bring it over." He handed her the cash and made his way over to his usual table. Immediately, his journal was on the table in front of him.

"You really don't go anywhere without that, do you?" Camille asked, placing a coffee and a muffin on his table.

"No, I don't." He saw she was hovering. "Do you want to sit down?" He indicated the empty chair opposite him.

"Sure. I'm due a break. Thanks." He shoved his backpack out of her way as she sat down. "So, is that like your bible or something?"

"More like a lifeline. It's like those diaries you see teenage girls writing in the movies."

"Oh, so it's your deepest, darkest thoughts?"

He liked the lightness to her voice despite the seriousness of the question.

"I guess. I just… every time something makes me feel, I write it in here."

"And do all these feelings become songs?" She looked genuinely interested in hearing what he had to say.

"Not all of them, but most of them. You gotta get it though, being a songwriter yourself."

"I do." Judging by the way she ducked her head to cut off eye contact, Ash wondered if he'd embarrassed her, and was about apologize when she spoke up. "I mean, it's crazy. I'm eighteen, I live in one of the most vibrant cities in the world, and my head sometimes feels like it's going to explode if I don't write things down to get them out."

Ash got it, more than she realized.

"Half the time," she continued. "not all of it makes any kind of sense. But getting them down onto paper just helps. Oh crap, sorry. I always say too much." She smiled at him, making him laugh softly.

"Don't apologize for being passionate, never to me at least."

"Thanks. I better get back. See you around."

Ash sure hoped so.

12

I t was raining as Ash sat on the windowsill of his bedroom looking out into the quiet street he'd grown up on. His parents were both at work, his friends at school, and he couldn't get out on the street to perform. For the first time in a long time, he felt lonely. It didn't happen very often, but when it did, it hit him hard. Abstractly, Ash knew he was a lucky kid. He had parents who accepted and loved him, despite their disagreements. He had two of the best friends anyone could want or need, and he had his music. His legacy. So why wasn't that enough sometimes? Why did it feel as if he were reaching for too much, that he wasn't good enough to achieve his dreams?

It was like something or someone was squeezing his heart and lungs when he felt this way and he never quite knew how to get the feeling to go away. His journal sat on his bed, but he had no motivation or inclination to write in it; his mood matched the weather outside and he hated it. Jumping to his feet, he picked up his acoustic and strummed a few chords. Even music couldn't pull him out of his funk, not least music he was struggling to write. Putting the guitar back on its stand, he went downstairs just for something to do. On the corner table in the hall he saw the key to the garage. Maybe a drive would help him clear his head.

Automatically, he packed up his guitar and carried it downstairs where he snatched up his keys and went out to his car. After stowing his guitar on the passenger seat, and strapping it in, he started the engine and pulled away from the house.

Although seeing the key to the garage had prompted his drive, he hadn't exactly planned to go there. He simply needed to get out of his bedroom, away from the invisible oppression that was making it hard for him to breathe. Anywhere had to be better than that, better than feeling as if he was drowning into his own mind and racing thoughts.

Letting himself into the studio, Ash slipped through the door without allowing the rain in. He laid his guitar case on the floor in front of the couch and flicked the stereo on. Instantly, the space around him filled with the sounds of Rush. He turned the volume down, so it was more background music and laid down on the couch and closed his eyes.

Although the vice-like feeling in his chest was still there, being in this space, so much like their old one and somewhere they could be themselves without fear of judgment, it was easing somewhat. If he was honest with himself, it never really went away; always lingering in the back of his mind, reminding him he was so insignificant in this city where everyone was trying to make a name for themselves. Hell, everyone in the country was like that with the rise of reality TV. He'd put so much stock in his music, the fear of failure and often crippling self-doubt were always there.

Without music, he was nothing, and people would know he was nothing. The moment he had his guitar in his hand, he felt visible and worthy. It was like a high he constantly chased, like an addict. He didn't necessarily want the attention the way Joey, and to some extent Chris did from the girls. It wasn't about *him;* Ash wanted his music to speak to people, for them to *feel* his music - Rare Breed's music. He couldn't begin to imagine what he would do if he didn't manage to achieve his dreams, even just part of the way; wouldn't imagine it.

As the music played in the background, Ash laid on the couch with his eyes closed trying not to spiral further. He needed to fight his way through the vice before it completely took ahold of him. It had only ever happened once, and it had caused a huge argument between him and his parents where he'd ended up living with Wes for almost a week. That was when he knew his parents regretted getting him a guitar as a kid and were disappointed he was never going to do the college thing. As an only child, there were expectations of him that he simply couldn't live up to, and no amount of pleading with him was ever going to change that.

:: ::

The sliding doors of the garage slamming together made Ash jolt upright. The music had stopped playing and he hadn't noticed. As he stood up to greet Wes and Chris, his journal and pen fell to the floor; he didn't even remember picking it up. His zoning out when he was feeling the way he was wasn't common, but it happened more than he liked.

"Hey, bro. How long you been here?" Chris asked him.

"I don't know. I needed to get out of my room, went for a drive and ended up here." Worry flashed across both of his friends faces. "I'm okay, honestly."

"You sure? You don't look it." Wes' voice was soft, as if he were speaking to a skittish kitten with razor sharp claws. With a groan, Ash walked into the bathroom and looked at his reflection in the mirror. Wes was right, he didn't look okay. His shaggy, light-brown hair was sticking out from under his beanie, his blue eyes were bloodshot, and there was stubble on his jaw that wasn't usually there. Another groan escaped as he splashed cool water onto his face and went back out to the guys.

"Do you think you should take a break? All

this rehearsing and the busking must be getting too much."

"Bro, thank you for worrying, but I'm fine. I'm just tired." He stood on his tiptoes and wrapped an arm around Chris' very slender shoulders and hugged him. He loved him like an annoying little brother and couldn't imagine life without him, without either of them. Wes joined in their hug and Ash felt the tell-tale prick of tears behind his closed eyelids.

"Of course, we worry about you, we all worry about each other. It's why we're bros. If it wasn't for you guys, my dad... well, yeah. I would be a constant bloody pulp, and Wes would probably still be in the closet. You guys are my family, the family I chose because you're fucking awesome." Chris' voice hitched and Ash tightened his hold on him.

Wes' phone ringing made them all step apart.

"Hey, Wyatt. Oh, okay. Give me a couple." He ended the call. "Wyatt's outside the gate. I invited him to watch us rehearse, is that all right with you two?"

"Bit late to say no now," Ash tormented, before smiling. "Go get your boy and we'll show him what you're made of."

Wes grinned and went rushing out of the studio.

:: ::

Rehearsal was shorter than usual because Chris had to go and help a neighbor he did jobs for. It was his only source of money to buy instruments or anything else he needed, so he did as much as he could. Plus, he was a genuinely nice guy who would give anyone the shirt off his back if they needed it. He also hid his money in a locked cash box in Ash's bedroom, knowing if he left it at home, his dad would somehow manage to break into it for booze. Once he left, there was no point in Wes and Wyatt staying, so Ash waved them off with a smile at their handholding as they let themselves out of the gate.

Once he was alone, he realized he felt better than he had, but not completely himself. That was the power of his friends and their music. They had always been able to bring him out of his own mind when it got too much for him. He knew if he didn't have them in his life, he probably wouldn't even have one.

13

I t took Ash a few days to fully feel like himself, but once he did, he threw himself into finding places for he and the guys to play some shows. The need to be on stage was like an itch you could never quite scratch because it moved around your body. His first port of call was the coffee house to speak to Leah.

"Hey, music man, long time no see," she greeted him. The coffee house was empty and she looked bored, something Ash was glad about.

"Hey, Leah, I was wondering if you knew of any venues that would let Rare Breed play a show or something. It doesn't need to be huge or anything. We just need to get back out there, know what I mean?"

"Yeah, I get it. I can't think of anything off the bat but leave it with me. I'll sort something out for you. Have you guys got Instagram and YouTube with videos and stuff on just in case I need to show anyone?" Nodding, Ash pulled his phone out of his pocket to show her so she could follow them on both. "Great. I already have your number, so I'll be in touch."

"Thanks so much, Leah. If you pull this off, I'll owe you big time."

"If I pull this off, I'll definitely be collecting. Double because of the garage."

Leaning over the counter, Ash planted a quick kiss on her cheek, making her laugh.

"I'll gladly pay anything," causing her to raise an eyebrow at him. "Leah, really? I'm not that kinda guy"

"Honey, you're pretty, but you ain't my type."

With a laugh, Ash left to set his gear up outside. He was in a good mood and it showed in his song choices. Green Day's *Burnout* – a classic as far as Ash was concerned, Weezer's *Buddy Holly* simply because the video was epic, and when he saw Camille approaching, he couldn't help but burst into *There She Goes* by The La's.

Upbeat 90s tracks mixed in with his own songs that made people walking past seem to smile a bit brighter after stopping and watching him for a few minutes. Ash felt great when he finished up and packed up. He put his guitar into the case without attempting to count the money that was in it.

As he was about to go to load up his trunk, Camille emerged from the coffee house, her shift over.

"Hey, you sounded really good today," she told him.

"Thanks. It was a good day."

"I could tell. You were extra bouncy while you were singing." That made Ash laugh. Wes always told him he was like a spring on stage. "Can I ask you something?"

"Sure."

"Why don't the guys ever play with you here? I mean, I know your drummer played that one song with you, but you always turn up on your own."

It was a fair question, and Ash was surprised no one had ever asked him it before.

"I'm mostly here while they're in school. When they let out, we rehearse in the studio, so they don't really have the chance most of the time."

"Oh, are you all still in high school and you just ditch to play music?"

"No, I graduated last year, but Chris and Wes are in their senior year."

"Didn't you want to go to college?" It was always the first question he was asked when people found out he was no longer in high school. It was exhausting even if he did understand.

"No. I'm not about the studying, I'm more about doing and forging my own future with my music." Camille didn't say anything for a while and Ash's arms were starting to ache from holding his collapsed mic stand, his guitar case, and his amp. "Look, I'm sorry, but this is getting heavy. I need to get it all in my trunk before my arms fall off. Do you need a ride anywhere?"

"Oh, that would be great. I'm actually heading over to my dad's, and from here it's an hour on the bus."

With a jerk of his head, he indicated for her to follow him to the parking lot where his car stuck out among all the shiny, new cars. "Wow, that's some car," Camille snorted as Ash unlocked the trunk and managed to put his stuff in.

"One, it's a classic, and two, it's all I can afford."

They climbed in and he started the engine. Immediately, the stereo kicked in, blasting out 5 Seconds of Summer's *Old Me*. "Shit, sorry." Ash fumbled to turn the music off.

"It's okay, at least I know you listen to something more current than 90s throwbacks."

"Hey, 90s throwbacks are awesome."

"Sure, if you say so."

"Camille Rogers, you clearly need a music education." Out of the corner of his eye, he saw her roll her eyes.

Silence fell over them as Ash drove through the sunlit street toward her house.

"You know, I admire you," Camille blurted out suddenly as they pulled onto her dad's street.

"Er, thanks. Why?"

"You're following your heart and chasing your dreams. Not many people do. Well, they chase what they *think* their dream is just to have their five minutes of fame. The passion you have for music is real."

Ash didn't know how to respond, but the

warmth he felt in his chest, where the vice grip usually had hold of him, made him smile at her.

"You're doing it too, just in a different way." He remembered what she'd told him about wanting to be a songwriter. "But why don't you want to be a performer when you're so fucking good at it?"

"It never called to me the way it does to you. I love singing, always will, but that's not my dream. I want to be that person who comes up with the perfect song that an artist can make their own and really convey a message to their fans. I want to be the heart of what they love to do."

"Wow. That's some poetic shit right there. I just know you're gonna meet those dreams and smash the industry into pieces." His words made her blush, again. Ash made it his life goal to bring that flush of color to her face every time they had a conversation because it was adorable as hell, and he couldn't stop his body reacting to it.

They'd been parked up in Mr. Rogers' drive for almost ten minutes before Camille realized where they were.

"Thanks for the ride, and the impressive compliments. See you around."

They both climbed out of the car and while

Ash made his way around the side of the house to the garage, Camille went straight up to the front door. Before he opened the gate, Ash looked over and caught her watching him.

She gave him a quick wave before letting herself into the house. Smiling and humming to himself, Ash continued on his way to the studio.

14

Leah had struck gold. Ash paced around his car, waiting for Wes and Chris to get out of school so he could tell them. He opened the text to read it again, excitement flowing through his entire body.

Saturday. Campus bar back room. Full set for you and a support. Paid.

The only issue was, he had no idea who they could get as a support act. He'd already responded to Leah's message asking if she knew anyone but hadn't had a reply. She was either at work or in class. It was frustrating the hell out of him.

Across the lot, he could see Wes and Chris

walking together and he jogged over to meet them.

"You look extra bouncy today." Wes noted as Ash thought back to Camille describing him in the same way. "What's got you so excited anyway?" he asked.

"Leah got us a gig. A *paid* gig."

Chris whooped as the three of them managed a messy trio high-five.

"Dude, that's epic. How many favors do you owe her now?" Chris asked as they reached the car and piled in.

"Two, and she's threatening to collect too. How the hell am I supposed to pay her back when I have nothing to offer?"

"We'll work it out, but first, tell us more about this show." Wes was the one able to prevent one of Ash's freak outs. His change of subject worked like a charm, and Ash told them all about the message he'd received from Leah.

"Boys, we need a set list." It felt like forever to him since they'd needed one, and he couldn't wait to work it out and add some of their new stuff.

"Our first proper show without Joey, gonna be weird." Chris commented from the back seat.

Ash agreed, it was going to be weird, but he felt they were so much better off without him.

"That new band he mentioned, it's with some kids at school. I've heard them practicing in one of the music rooms at lunch. They're okay, theirs is heavier than our stuff, but hell. We all know Joey's an incredible pianist."

"Shame he can't write songs for shit though," Ash spat out, still pissed at their former friend and bandmate.

"Yeah, this guy's our secret weapon on that front." He patted Ash's shoulder. "It's like your superpower, bro. I wish I could see the world the way you do."

"You really don't. Ash is way too cynical for you. You're too pure to be subjected to the way his mind works," Wes told the youngest of their trio, making his pale cheeks flood with red.

"I'm not sure if that's an insult or a compliment."

"Take it as you wish, Ashley." From the back of the car, Chris barked out a laugh.

"I hate you guys sometimes."

"Ashley Kane, you liar. You love us and couldn't be without us." Wes' voice was completely deadpan.

"Ain't that the truth."

:: ::

It took Rare Breed three days to pin down their final set list for their show. On the fourth, Ash found himself alone in the studio. Chris was out helping another neighbor mow some grass and trim some topiaries as he needed some new leads for his amp. Wes had gone to meet Wyatt from work. Between Wyatt's part-time job in a surf store near the beach and Wes still being in high school, they didn't get to spend much time together.

So, Ash made the most of having the space to himself now he was able to handle his own company, and work on some new songs that had been floating around in his head.

"Hey, Ash. You in here?" Ben stuck his head through the gap in the sliding doors.

"Yeah, little dude, I'm here. What's up?"

"Nothing, I just wanted to show you how much better I'm getting at those exercises you showed me last week. If you're not too busy."

Ash grinned at Camille's brother, as he closed his journal.

"I'm all yours, man. Show me what you got."

Ben sat down on a chair facing the couch. A look of concentration appeared on his face as he positioned the guitar he'd recently replaced the loan from Ash with, and began to play. It was only chords, and he got most of them right, so Ash was pleased for the kid. Over the next couple of hours, he spent his time making sure Ben's fingers were positioned correctly over the frets and he was holding down the right strings. The kid was a quick study and was soon playing a rendition of one of the first songs Ash had ever learned to play, *Happy Birthday.*

"Ben, you still out here?" Mr. Rogers' voice called out from just outside the doors of the garage.

"Yeah, Dad. In here."

Mr. Rogers walked in, smiling when he saw his son with the guitar in his hands and Ash kneeling on the floor in front of him.

"How are the lessons going?" he asked as Ben continued to practice.

"He's doing great, better than me when I first started."

"Yeah, I don't believe you. You're awesome

on the guitar," Ben told him once he finished and packed his stuff away.

"That's only because I practiced all the time. My mom nearly threw that thing away after I made my fingers bleed. I don't recommend that by the way, but an hour a day, and you'll soon be shredding with me and the boys." Ash's heart clenched a little at the wide smile on the younger Rogers' face. He'd always wanted a younger sibling for moments just like this.

"That would be *awesome.* I could join your band."

"Maybe, little dude." He grinned.

"Okay, Ben, go and put that away and wash up for dinner." With a cheery goodbye, the kid ran out through the doors and up to the house. "Thank you, Ash. I've not seen him so happy in a long time."

"It's a pleasure Mr. Rogers. He's gonna be good."

Ash felt uncomfortable around Camille's dad, not because there was something off about him, but because he was so accepting of everything. He'd never met a nicer man, who took everything in his stride with a smile on his face.

"Please, call me Harry. I think you've earned

it. Would you like to join us for dinner? It's only reheated spaghetti."

"Uhm... sure." He followed the older man out of the garage, locking the door, and up to the house.

Ben was already sitting at the table chatting away to Camille about what he'd learned that afternoon.

"Hey."

:: ::

It was almost midnight when Leah finally got back to him with her suggestion for a support act. When he read her message, he couldn't help but grin into his pillow. Camille Rogers was going to perform before Rare Breed.

I thought she didn't want to be a performer. He replied once he was able to control himself.

She doesn't, but she still loves to sing and get feedback on her songs.

Well, that made sense.

Just let me know the run times etc before Saturday so I can prep the guys.

You got it, music man.

He enjoyed Leah's nickname for him; it made him feel validated. Putting his phone back on his nightstand, he lay on his back looking up at his ceiling which was lit up by the sliver of moonlight coming through the crack in his drapes. He couldn't wait to watch Camille on stage again and he hoped she would stay to watch their set so he could have the chance to impress her with more than his busking skills.

Imagining her dancing to music he wrote was a huge turn on for Ash, and it didn't take long for his body to be as awake as his mind. Turning his head slightly, he made sure his bedroom door was completely closed before pushing his hands past the waistband of his boxers and gripping hold of himself. He stroked his cock with a firm grip while thinking of the barista who'd captured his heart, picturing her bright eyes and wide smile.

15

Ash's dad drove them to the venue, their gear once again in the borrowed neighbor's trailer. He even helped them unload everything and carry it all inside. He didn't help them set up because he was scared he'd break something.

"Would you guys mind if I stayed for the show?" he asked once they had finished and were chilling out in a tiny room that was acting like a green room for them. Ash was shocked but grinned at his dad.

"Dad, that would be awesome." Neither of his parents had watched one of their shows in far too long, and the idea of his dad watching this one lit him up. Ash had noticed that lately, his dad had shown more interest in his music, whereas before it was more indifference.

"Let me just go and call your mom, let her know. I'll be the old guy at the back of the room." He grinned at them before ducking out, his cell phone in his hand.

"Uh, Ash. When did you dad become cool?" Chris asked, looking at the door that was now closed. "I mean, he's always been cool with me, but this... this is new. Isn't it?"

"Bro, I'm just as confused as you. It's like, ever since Joey quit, my dad's become so supportive of me and all this. It's weird, but I'm just going with it. Makes my life at home so much easier."

"I'm glad. At least one of us is happy at home," Wes spoke from where he stood across the room, leaning up against the wall.

"What's up?" Ash asked concerned.

"Nothing new."

Before any of them could speak, there was a knock on the door. When Chris pulled it open, Leah was on the other side.

"Boys, we have a packed house out there. Camille goes on in fifteen for her five songs, then the stage is all yours. Make momma proud." The boys jumped up and pulled Leah into a messy group hug, making her laugh before shoving them all away. "Is that what you're all wearing?" She looked the three of them up and down, taking in the skinny jeans, sneakers, and the rest of their clothes.

"Hey, what's wrong with what we're wearing?" Chris tugged at his leather jacket, the one and only decent birthday present from his parents. The rest of his clothes were less refined, but he didn't particularly care.

"If that's the look y'all are going for, have at it." She flicked her long hair over her shoulder. "You're all the rock stars, not me. Speaking of, I need you all to sign these. We have a bunch of people asking for them." She thrust a large pile of the posters she'd had made up for the show. Their band logo was front and center on the black background.

"Wait, people want our autographs?" Chris asked, dumbfounded as Ash took the posters and some sharpies from Leah who slipped out of the room with a smile. "My God, people *want* our autographs. I can't breathe." He started to hyperventilate making his bandmates panic. Rushing over to him, Wes led Chris over to a chair and pushed him to sit down.

"Dude, relax. It's all cool. All you need to do is sign your name without spelling it wrong," Ash told him, handing over a silver sharpie. He felt bad for saying it, but he'd needed to snap his friend out of it.

"We're screwed, because I can't remember how to spell my name right now."

"Well, you have less than a half hour to remember." Ash told him as he signed the first poster and passed it along to Wes.

When they were finished, Ash took the top three off the pile, rolled them up and put them into his backpack.

"These are ours for the studio, our first ever signed merch. We're on the way, boys." The three of them piled on top of one another, landing on the couch in a tangle of arms, legs, and laughter. "Let's go give these to Leah, then watch Camille's set."

"I need to see if Wyatt's here yet." Wes led the way out of the room and into the venue which was packed with bodies.

Chris grabbed hold of Ash's arm and hissed.

"Dude, look how many people are here. To

see *us*. This is insane." Ash could hear the hysteria building in Chris' voice again and squeezed his hand in an attempt to reassure him as Wes looked for Wyatt.

They found Wyatt at the door with Leah. Ash handed over the posters as Wes introduced his boyfriend to everyone. While they were talking, the singer felt a warm hand on his shoulder and turned to find his dad behind him. In the excitement, he'd forgotten he was still there. His dad jerked his head, indicating for them to follow him. Once they were free of the crowd, the three bandmates and Wyatt waited for Ash's dad to speak.

"I wanted to tell you boys how proud I am of you, all of you. You're all insanely talented and I know you're going to blow all of these people away." He drew the three boys in for a hug as Ash felt tears prick at his eyes. His dad had finally told him, them, he was proud of what he was doing.

"Thanks Mr. Kane, means a lot." Chris' face was bright red and his voice was thick with emotion. Wes merely hugged the older man again, not needing to say anything.

"Mr. Kane, can you do me a favor? This is my

boyfriend, Wyatt. Will you look after him while we're on stage?" He pulled Wyatt closer with a tug on his hand.

"Wes, it would be my honor."

"What's up everyone?" Leah's voice filled the entire room as she walked onto stage with a microphone in her hand. "Who's ready for some *epic* live music?" A cheer from the crowd almost deafened Ash and brought a wide smile to his face. He could already feel the electricity in the atmosphere and his entire body was tingling from it. "I know most of you are here to see Rare Breed, and they'll be on later, but first it's my girl, the crazy talented Camille Rogers."

Ash's breath caught in his throat as Camille walked out onto the stage holding a guitar and then sat behind the piano.

"I'm gay, and even I can see she looks hot," Wes murmured in his ear.

Ash couldn't respond.

:: ::

Watching Camille on stage was almost a religious experience for Ash. Not only was her voice incredible, but her lyrics were insightful and heartbreaking all at the same time. Chris and Wes had to physically drag him away so they could get ready to perform themselves.

"Come on, Romeo. If you stay there, we'll have to find a new lead singer." Chris yanked on his arm. Eventually, Ash pulled his eyes away from the girl on stage and followed his bandmates.

"Dude, you're drooling." Wes threw a paper towel at him.

"No, I'm not." Ash wiped at his mouth, just to be sure, making his friends laugh.

"There's serious droolage, buddy. But we'll let you off, because that girl is kinda amazing." Chris nudged him with his shoulder, his green eyes twinkling under the lights.

"Shut up. Band circle."

The three of them joined hands and pressed their heads together. None of them needed to say anything, they all felt it.

"After tonight, everything changes." He squeezed both of their hands. "This is just the first step on the ladder, boys. Now, let's rock this. 'Rock out' on three," they put their hands in the center of their circle. "One, two, three…"

"Rock out."

16

W alking out onto a stage wasn't a new
experience for any of them, but not
only were they following the powerhouse that
was Camille Rogers, but the room was full of
people who wanted to see them. They weren't
there for the main act and having to put up with
Rare Breed as a warmup; they *were* the main act
and that blew his mind.

"Let's get started. We're Rare Breed and this
is *Dirty Weekend.*" Ash introduced the band and
they started straight in with the music, the reason
they were there, the reason he was able to
breathe.

Their fifteen-song set flew past, and it was
soon time for their final song. *Lost in Translation*

was a favorite of theirs to perform, but after the YouTube video, it seemed to be a crowd favorite as the people in front of them went insane as soon as the intro started. As he sang, Ash couldn't help but notice some of the audience singing along. Strangers knew the lyrics to one of his songs and it was seriously blowing his mind. He looked over at Chris and could see the same look of complete bewilderment on the bassist's face.

The applause when they finished was deafening and the three of them lapped it up as they took their end of show bow and ran off the stage.

"Oh. My. God." Wes was pacing back and forth, his face flushed, his eyes bright, and the widest smile Ash had seen on his face for a long time.

Before either he or Chris could respond, Ash's dad and Wyatt joined them.

"Boys, that was incredible." Mr. Kane pulled the three of them into a group hug while Wyatt watched with a smile on his face.

"You really think so?" Ash asked him, suddenly feeling a little unsure of himself despite the adrenaline surging through him.

"Ash, you boys were electric up there. The three of you were born for performing, and you...

your lyrics are inspired." Rather than say anything, Ash threw his arms around his dad's neck, needing to stand on his tiptoes to make sure he could reach as tears began to roll down his face.

"Mr. Kane, you're pretty cool, you know that?" Chris asked as he joined in, Wes soon following.

"Let me go and get the car, so you can load everything up before mingling with a huge crowd of people who want to meet you." He left the three friends and Wyatt alone. The surfer approached them slowly, as if unsure whether he should intrude on their moment together.

"He's right you know. You guys were awesome." He spoke softly, making the three of them turn to face him. Ash's hand squeezed at Wes' before he gave his drummer a subtle nod of his head. At Ash's signal, Wes let go of his friends and flew into Wyatt's arms.

"We'll just..." Chris and Ash left the couple alone for privacy and went to begin packing up their gear.

:: ::

Ash's dad had driven their gear back home and had left the guys to stay at the venue for a while to revel in the attention they were receiving from the audience. As they were approached by yet more girls, Ash could see Leah and Camille out of the corner of his eye sitting in a corner of the venue.

"Excuse me, I've just got to..." He squeezed through the group, leaving Chris to turn up his adorable charm while Wes and Wyatt watched amused.

"Hey."

Leah and Camille looked up at him, smiling.

"Music man, just the singer I needed to see. I have something for you." Leah searched through the backpack at her feet and withdrew an envelope. "This is for you guys. Your fee plus a portion of ticket sales. You earned it tonight, and I've already been asked when you're next playing and for all of your social media handles. Expect plenty of new follow-ers." She excused herself and made her way over to the makeshift bar. Ash slid into her empty seat; the envelope gripped tightly in his hand.

"I'm glad Leah made me stay, you guys are

fantastic, but I'm sure you've heard that a lot tonight," Camille told him.

"We have, but somehow it's different hearing it from you." Ash cursed the low lighting; he couldn't tell if she was blushing or not.

"Yeah, and why's that?"

"Because, Camille Rogers, you have a sledge-hammer of a voice and write amazing songs. To have someone with your insane talent compliment us, it means something. It's not empty platitudes or girls saying what they think we want to hear in the hopes of a hook up."

Her face scrunched up at that, he definitely noticed that.

"Not that any of us would do that... well, Chris might, but Chris has always been a bit of a tramp." Ash looked over to his redheaded friend who was deep in conversation with a girl with bright blue hair, trying not to laugh at the way they clashed.

"Well, thank you for the compliments. I enjoyed playing tonight."

"You should do it more, it's clear you have the passion for it."

"I don't mind doing something now and then, but-"

"Yeah, it's not the end goal. I have to say, I think you're insane and wasting your talent. But I also respect your dreams."

Silence fell over them as they both looked out across the thinning crowd. Ash watched Chris luck out with the blue-haired girl as Wes and Wyatt looked to be in their own bubble of happiness, whispering into one another's ears with sappy smiles on their faces.

"I guess I best get back to my dorm, I have an early shift at work tomorrow." Camille stood up slowly. Ash really didn't want her to leave but knew he couldn't stop her. "I just need to find Leah."

"Oh, she told me to pass a message onto you." Chris appeared beside them. "She said that she needed to book and would meet you back at your dorm."

"Translation, she met a guy. Great." Camille sank back down onto her chair. "I hate walking home alone. I guess I'll order an Uber." She slid her phone out of her bag.

"I'll walk you back," Ash blurted out, causing Chris to snort behind him. A swift kick to the shin put a stop to that.

"I can't ask you to do that, you need to get

back yourself."

"You're not asking, I'm offering. Let me just grab my backpack." He jogged over to where Wes and Wyatt were still cocooned in one another's arms. "Hey, guys, you go without me. I'm gonna make sure Camille gets back safe, then I'll jump in an Uber home. I'll meet you at the studio in the morning to split our money."

He shoved the envelope into his backpack and pulled it onto his shoulder.

"Yeah, I'm sure you'll get home tonight..." Wyatt teased, earning an elbow to the ribs from Wes.

"I'll be the perfect gentleman." Ash saluted the couple before going back to join Camille. "Hey, you going to my place?" Chris nodded. "Okay, here's the key. Please be quiet going in, I'll meet you back there."

Chris took the keys and gave Ash a swift, one-armed hug before returning to Wes.

"Are you sure about this?" Camille asked him as she picked up her guitar case.

"Positive." Ash took the guitar from her and slung it over his shoulder with his bag and the two of them walked out into the cool night. "Lead on."

17

New York City is known as the city that never sleeps, but Ash had noticed that Los Angeles was rarely silent in the evenings. The stores may be closed and very few tourists around, but the clubs, bars, and late-night bodegas were open and drew in people constantly.

As he and Camille walked away from the campus bar, he noticed students wandering around, some with their arms full of books from the library, others in groups laughing and joking. Watching her out of the corner of his eye, he could see she was completely at home in these surroundings. Ash had never felt more out of place and he didn't know how to deal with it.

"Why do you live on campus even though your house isn't far?"

"When I was younger, I'd always planned to go to college in New York, but after my mom left us, I wanted to stay close to my dad and Ben in case they needed me, but Dad insisted I have the full college experience by living on campus with Leah. We just have the added security blanket of being able to go home if we need to. Plus, my aunt checks up on us now and then as she works nearby, makes sure we're eating properly and using the right detergent on our clothes." She let out a low laugh.

"Your family are really important to you, aren't they?"

"Aren't yours? I saw you with your dad tonight, you look close."

"We're getting there. It's been... tough, but things are changing."

"For the good?" When Ash nodded, she smiled. "I'm glad."

The conversation dried up as they walked and Ash scrambled to think of something to say, but before he could, Camille came to a stop outside a huge building.

"This is me." She looked down at her feet, her long hair falling over her face.

"I'll walk you to the door, make sure you get inside safely." Ash held his arm out, indicating for her to lead the way. Which she did, with a smile. Sooner than he'd like, they were hovering by the door into the building.

"Well, I guess I better head in." Camille shuffled her feet against the sidewalk.

"Oh, shit. Here. This is yours." Ash was so used to having a guitar slung over a shoulder, he'd forgot he was carrying it for her.

"Thanks. Look, you guys really were amazing tonight. I can imagine you playing somewhere like Madison Square Garden, and then on to dominate the world."

"Wow, hell of an endorsement there. Thank you."

Without warning, Camille leaned forward and placed a kiss on his cheek.

"Thank you for walking me home." She turned on her heel and walked inside the building, Ash watching unable to say anything even if he wanted to. Once she was out of sight, he let out a quiet 'whoop' before pulling his phone out and ordering an Uber.

:: ::

Hoping Chris was still awake when he got home, he stood under his window and called Chris' phone rather than ringing the bell and waking his parents.

"What's up, bro?" Chris asked, his voice sounding sleepy.

"Dude, you're in my house and I can't get in. Throw me down my keys."

He could hear rustling from the other end of the call before it cut off. Then Chris' pale face appeared at his window as he threw Ash his keys.

"So, how did it go?" Chris asked the minute Ash closed his bedroom door behind him, giving his blond eyebrows a wiggle.

"I walked her home, that's it." Turning his back on his friend so he wouldn't have to look at his face, Ash kicked off his shoes and dropped his hoodie on the back of his chair.

"I saw the way you were looking at her, something I haven't seen in a long time by the way, and I know you like her. A lot." Ash sighed as he turned to sink onto his bed. "Wow, I never thought I'd see the day Ashley Kane was hung up on a girl."

"Shut up."

Ash was used to teasing Chris about girls, and it felt weird having it done back to him. Chris was right, Ash didn't get hung up on girls; his focus was always on the music and the band. It was all he needed to concentrate on. He was only eighteen, the whole relationship thing could come later once he'd begun to make his mark.

"Seriously though, bro, why are you so... hesitant about all this? She seems cool and we already know her family and friends, so I don't get it."

Leaning back against his headboard, Ash thought about Chris' question. He didn't have a definitive answer, not really.

"Actually, I do get it. You're scared."

"Chris-"

"No wait, hear me out." Chris held his hand up. Ash stayed quiet because it wasn't often that his friend wasn't as clueless as people thought he was. "For the last three years, you've been all tunnel vision about Rare Breed, even more since you graduated. We all want the band to be big, but you take it to extremes most of the time. Then this girl comes along, gets your attention without even trying, and you don't know how to deal with it. You're usually the one brushing girls off at shows, but this time you're the one who's interested."

Ash was speechless. Chris was supposed to be the dork of their group, the one who had no idea about girls – which was why he always lucked out with them – but this. This was different; insightful.

"And, for the record. I approve." Chris leaned back on his elbows looking proud of himself.

"Thanks, buddy."

"So, when are you gonna ask her out? Do the whole dating thing like a normal person?"

"Hey! I *am* a normal person, Christian."

"Sure, whatever."

Silence filled the room as Chris made himself comfortable on the airbed and soon fell asleep. Ash stripped down to his boxers and climbed under his covers, but his body was still on overdrive, not only from the show but from the innocent kiss Camille had placed on his cheek.

Was Chris right? Was he scared of the whole dating thing? If he was honest with himself, which didn't happen particularly often, he was. Maybe it was time to take the blinkers off and let his life revolve around something other than music for a while.

:: ::

The following morning, Ash and Chris climbed into Ash's car and drove over to pick Wes up. It was time for the full Rare Breed line-up to put on a show outside *Downtown Beans*. He didn't feel as if he needed to hide the coffee house from his friends now they knew about Camille. At least he didn't have to put up with Joey and his little passive aggressive comments anymore. Now they weren't friends, Ash could look back on the last three years and realize that Joey had always been the one who pushed Ash to concentrate on the music side of things, feeding into his hunger as if he didn't want competition with the girls who were showing them interest after shows and at school.

Before they set up, they went inside to order a coffee each and to work out a set list. Neither Leah nor Camille were working, and Brian had an odd look on his face as he served Ash, who paid with their earnings from the previous evening.

"Thanks, Brian, have a nice day." He was in a good mood and some stuck-up coffee house assistant manager wasn't going to ruin it. Carrying three steaming hot drinks wasn't easy but he managed it without spilling any of them.

"So, boys. What are we singing today?" he asked, sitting down and glancing out of the window into the glorious sunshine. There should be a lot of people milling around the sidewalk, which made his adrenaline spike. Ash thrived on performing, regardless of where. Ideas for songs came from both sides of him and they worked together to build up a comprehensive set list.

Ash was in his happy place with his best friends, his brothers, his family.

18

Halfway through their set, the boys took a break and Wes ran inside to get them drinks and snacks. Camille and Leah had arrived for work ten minutes after they'd begun, and Ash could see them chatting to Wes as he waited for his order.

"What's with all the 90s alt rock? I mean, I know you're a fan, but you usually mix it up much more than this," Chris asked.

"I was just in the mood for some throwbacks."

"Okay. Sure."

Wes re-joined them, handing out drinks and muffins.

"Camille asked me to pass on a message." He

144

looked directly at Ash.

"Oh?"

"This century." Chris looked confused at their conversation, but Ash didn't explain, knowing Wes knew what was happening.

"Is that it?"

"That's it. I think I have an idea what she means, and I'm not getting involved." The drummer sat back on his cajon and ate his muffin while Ash turned to the window and looked in at Camille. When she caught his eye, he raised his cup up in a 'cheers' motion and grinned. There was no way in hell he was stopping the 90s tracks today. It was too much fun knowing that not only was Camille paying attention to what they were playing, but he was getting a reaction from her.

"I'm just going to the restroom, boys, then we can do some more. Pickings are good today." He indicated the guitar case that was filling up nicely with cash. Wes had been removing the notes to prevent them being blown away or potentially stolen. Ash drained his drink and went inside.

"If you've come to argue the merits of 90s alt rock, you can keep moving," Camille spoke without looking up from the coffee machine she was operating. With a chuckle, Ash kept walking through to the customer restroom.

"Hey, music man." Leah called out once he'd finished up. He went over to the hatch to the small kitchen. "She loves Bon Jovi. Just saying."

The grin on his face was so wide, it made his cheeks ache; even more so when Camille gave him a look that could only be described as 'side eye'. Unable to stop himself, he winked at her as he walked past, taking a smug satisfaction when she fumbled the cash she had just been handed, spilling it all over the floor. Well, he was sorry she dropped the money, but pleased she had a reaction to him to cause her to do it.

"What's up next?" Chris consulted the set list they had worked on as Ash re-joined them.

"*Old Before my Time.*"

"Either of you mind if we skip it? I've had a request from Leah."

"Sure, what does she want to hear?"

"*You Give Love A Bad Name.*"

"Yes, a bit of Jovi. Thank you, Leah." Chris bounced on his heels as Wes laughed at him before counting the two of them in.

Ash's strong and clear voice filled the air outside *Downtown Beans* as the three of them rocked out. It didn't take long for a crowd to surround them, joining in with the chorus and throwing money into Ash's guitar case. Loud applause erupted the moment they finished and the three of them took a bow before launching immediately into another of their own songs.

:: ::

Once they'd finished, split their earnings, and packed their gear away in the trunk of Ash's car, Wes disappeared to go and meet Wyatt.

"I gotta go, I'm babysitting for Mr. and Mrs. Miller tonight." Chris told Ash as they walked back toward the coffee house. His neighbors had twin four-year-old boys, and from what Ash knew about them, the boys adored Chris and he babysat for them once a month.

"Do you need a ride?"

"Nah, they've ordered me an Uber as part of my payment."

"Okay, bro. Let me know if you need me at all." As Chris' Uber pulled up, they bumped fists. After watching the car drive away, Ash decided to go and have a panini and see if Camille was still working.

When he walked inside, a couple of girls giggled as he moved past their table. He was almost at the counter when one of them called out to him.

"You were awesome out there today."

Ash turned with a wide smile on his face.

"Thanks." His single word caused more giggles and with a shake of his head, he continued on his path to the counter where Leah was watching him. "What?"

"Nothing, music man, nothing at all." Without taking his order, she began to prepare the black coffee he always ordered.

"Yeah, like you ever have nothing to say."

Before she could respond further than the eyeroll she aimed at him, Ash felt a tap on his shoulder. Turning, he saw the two girls standing behind him.

"Can we have a selfie with you?"

Leah snorted out a laugh behind him as he agreed and let the girls stand either side of him, holding an iPhone in a bright pink case to snap a couple of photos. They said their thanks and scuttled away, giggling once more. Ash wasn't sure, but he thought one of them squealed about him being 'so hot' as they left *Downtown Beans.*

"Oh my god, you're totally gonna be riding on that for at least a month, aren't you?" Leah placed his drink on the counter in front of him, holding her hand out for his money.

"I would never." Ash feigned offence but couldn't quite wipe the smile off his face as he paid.

"I may not have known you that long, or even know you that well, but believe me when I say I know this. You loved every minute of that."

"Well, it wasn't a bad experience, that's for sure."

The coffee house was quiet, so rather than go and sit at his usual table, Ash hovered at the counter to chat with Leah. They traded barbs as Leah worked and Ash drank hot coffee.

"So, when are you gonna ask?" Leah blurted out after almost a half hour of banter between them.

"Ask what?"

"About Camille." Her bluntness made him choke on the mouthful of hot panini he'd just taken.

"What about her?"

"You must think I'm an idiot or something. Anyone with eyes can see how much you like

149

her. All she has to do is breathe and your heart eyes go crazy."

"I don't have 'heart eyes'."

"You keep telling yourself that. Look, my girl Camille is quite possibly the best person I know, and she deserves to be happy. I've seen the way you look at her, like you'd worship her, and I've seen the way she looks at you right back."

"How... how does she look at me?" He just *had* to know, even if it made him look a little desperate.

"Why are guys so damn oblivious?" Leah muttered to herself as she served a customer behind him. Standing to one side, Ash waited so they could finish their interesting conversation. "When you guys were on stage the other night, she couldn't keep her eyes off you, and whenever you set up outside, there's a little smile on her face. Do me a favor and just ask her out already."

He didn't know how to respond to that order, so he simply took a bite of his panini as Leah looked at him.

"You're scared to, aren't you?" She actually giggled at the idea. "Music man, I never thought you, the guy who struts around like he owns the place and performs music as if he's destined to be a star, would be scared to ask a girl out on a date."

"It's not that I'm scared... I just, I haven't dated in a while. Most girls don't appreciate playing second best to my music and me trying to make myself a better artist. At first, it's all 'I'm with the band' and bragging to friends, but rehearsals, gigs, and writing, soon becomes old real quick. My drive and chasing my dreams aren't exactly conducive to a healthy relationship, so I don't date."

"You *have* been with a girl though, right?"

He glared at her. "Really? You're asking me this, in public? Yes, I have, not that it's anything to do with you."

"Well, I gotta check. Not gonna lie, seeing you and your boys perform, there's some serious chemistry between you and Chris on stage when you share a mic." Ash snorted. "What?"

For a split second, Ash debated telling her, but decided against it. His history with Wes had nothing to do with this conversation.

"That's all part of the show."

"Look, you're a good-looking guy and you know *exactly* how to use that when you sing. You ooze this confidence that is important for a front man to have, so why not filter that through into real life a bit?"

"Aww, you think I'm good looking. You going soft on me there, Leah?"

"Don't flutter those puppy-dog eyes at me. Go ask Camille out. She's at her dad's and believe me when I say this... she'll say yes."

"Why should I believe you?"

"You're not bad to look at and you're teaching her brother how to play the guitar. Believe me, she's hella interested."

With a dismissive wave of her hand, Ash was under orders. Would he have the balls to follow them?

19

A sh sat opposite Ben as the younger boy played *Happy Birthday* flawlessly.

"Yes, little dude. That was awesome." He held his hand up for a high-five; the slap resounded around the garage.

"You really think so?" Ben asked, uncertainty in his voice.

"Yes, I really think so. You have a natural talent." The smile that lit up Ben's face was wide, and Ash remembered how it felt when he was learning and nailed a piece of music his teacher had instructed him to learn.

Wes entered the garage with Chris clinging to his back. Ash didn't ask, but he was sure his face said it all.

"Chris saw a spider."

"Dude, it had my name tattooed on its knuckles and wore combat boots." Chris slid off Wes' back and pulled the doors to the garage closed behind them.

"It was a garden spider, nothing too crazy." Wes told Ash, making Ben laugh. "Barely even worth calling a spider really."

Chris watched the two of them, horror written all over his face, before stalking away muttering to himself.

"You good for today, little dude?" Ash asked Ben who was putting his guitar into its case carefully.

"Yeah, thanks." After a round of fist bumps, Camille's brother left the garage.

"Have you seen the lovely Ms. Rogers yet to ask her out?" Wes asked, sitting on the couch next to Ash.

"No."

"Well, we just saw her going into the house. So, go do it, do the thing. I need to run out and meet Wyatt at work so he can come and watch us rehearse."

Both of them looked over to where Chris was plucking at his bass, still sulking about the spider.

"You wanna come with, bro?" Wes asked him.

"Nah, I need to retune this bad boy. I'll wait here because I'm sure Ash doesn't want an audience."

"I do not. But I need an excuse to be going up to the house though. I can't just head up and be all 'oh hey, wanna go out?', can I?"

"Sure you can. It's not rocket science. All you need to do is ask her out, decide on a time and boom! Date sorted. I'll be back in a half hour." Wes slid the doors open, making Chris squeak as he pulled his feet off the floor.

"He's right, you know." Chris said when they were alone. "You're overthinking all this." Chris told Ash as he put his head in his hands. Why was this so hard?

"I know he is, and I don't know why I'm finding this so crazy hard, but I am."

"Ash. You spend so much time trying to plan everything to do with your music and the band, but you need to remember you're still only eighteen and need to have an actual life too. Now, get off your tuckus and go and get the girl."

"Tuckus? Really?"

Chris just grinned at him as he stood up,

determined to ask Camille out. "Oh, on your way out, can you close the doors, just in case the spider decides to come and eat me?" With a snort, Ash left the garage, sliding the doors closed behind him.

Walking through the yard, he ran a few scenarios over in his mind. What if she said no? What if she laughed at him? What if she said yes, and expected the full works of a fancy meal? Chris was right, he was overthinking this. Camille didn't seem like the kind of girl who would expect an all-out date at a top restaurant. She came across as more of a quiet walk along the beach before having something like tacos under the pier, the intimate and friendly kind of dates.

Sooner than he liked, he was at the kitchen door and hesitating. Inside, he could hear Ben playing the guitar, strains of the only song he knew filtering out to Ash. With a grin, he raised his hand and knocked on the door. Through the glass, he saw Camille walking through the kitchen toward him, making his heart pound. He was really about to do this, wasn't he?

"Hey, Ash." Her smile was wide, and he couldn't help but smile back. "Ben was just showing off his skills. You must be a great teacher to have patience with my little brother."

"It's all on him, he has an ear. Must run in the family." His compliment made her blush and Ash couldn't help but mentally pat himself on the back. "Look, I was wondering something."

"Oh?"

Camille stood to one side to let him enter the kitchen where the smell of spaghetti sauce hung in the air, making his stomach rumble.

"Do you want some food? Dad always makes too much, and we end up eating leftovers for days; drives my aunt crazy."

"No, thanks. I'm good. I was just wondering-" He finally had the courage to say the words, but before he could. Chris rushed into the kitchen, his red hair sticking up as if he'd been running his hands through it. His face was flushed and he was waving his phone in his hand.

"Sorry to disturb, but Ash I need you. Wes is hurt."

:: ::

Ash gripped the steering wheel so hard, his knuckles turned white as he drove to the beach.

Chris was on the phone to Wyatt trying to work out exactly where they were while directing Ash.

"There they are." Ash didn't need Chris to point as he pulled up behind a cop car and an ambulance. The two of them climbed out of his car and ran over to where their friend was sat on a gurney being treated for a gash above his eye and a split lip.

"Wyatt, what the hell happened?" Ash asked, unable to take his eyes off his best friend and ex.

"We were just heading back to the garage for your rehearsal and four guys started yelling shit at us, calling us fags and other names. When Wes ignored them, they jumped us. He pushed me out of the way and took the worst of it."

Looking at Wyatt, he could see the surfer had a few grazes on his hands, but other than that, he looked okay.

"Is he gonna be all right?" Chris asked, his voice small. Ash wrapped an arm around his shoulders and pulled him tight against him. Chris didn't like physical fights and with the way his dad was, Ash didn't blame him.

"Where are the guys?"

"Three of them ran off, but some surfer

buddies helped me grab the fourth one." Wyatt pointed to the cop car where a guy was hand-cuffed in the back. Letting go of Chris, Ash started to stalk over to him, but Chris grabbed hold of the shirt he wore, pulling him back.

"Do you want to get arrested too?" he hissed into Ash's ear.

"I don't fucking care, I want to kill him."

"Dude. I do too but let the police deal with him. We've got Wes to worry about." The mention of their friend shook Ash's focus away from the guy in the back of the police car and back onto the gurney in front of them.

"We're going to have to take him for stitches and an X-ray. Who's coming with him?"

Ash ushered Wyatt into the ambulance to sit next to the gurney, promising to meet them at the hospital. Once the doors had been slammed closed, he and Chris went back to his car and climbed in. As soon as the ambulance pulled away, Ash followed it, determined not to be sepa-rated from it.

:: ::

It took three hours for Wes to be discharged

into the care of Ash's mom and dad. They'd phoned Wes' parents and got their permission for him to stay at their house while he recovered from his cracked rib and facial injuries at both boys requests. When the doctor signed his papers, Ash saw a tightness around the man's eyes as he spoke to Wes' dad.

Driving Wes, Wyatt, and Chris back to his house, Ash let his anger flow through him. Anger at Wes getting hurt, at him and Wyatt's being victims of a hate crime, and most of all, anger at Wes' parents giving up on their son so easily when he needed them the most. It didn't matter if he wanted to go home or not, they should have fought for the safety of their son.

"Right, Wes you're not going to be able to sleep on the air bed, so I'll make up the spare room for you. I'll get your pain meds ready while you get changed." Ash's mom pressed a kiss to the boy's forehead before disappearing into the kitchen. Ash nodded at his dad as the three of them helped Wes get upstairs and into Ash's bedroom where he kept some clothes.

"Thanks, guys," he croaked out, wincing in pain as he lowered himself onto the chair at Ash's desk.

"Buddy, there's no need to thank us. You know that."

"There is." Wincing again, Wes yawned.

"Come on, let's get you changed and into bed. Wyatt, you can stay with him if you want." Ash turned to the fourth of their group who was standing in the corner watching them.

"If that's what Wes wants, otherwise I can leave you all to it." The surfer looked unsure and worried.

"No. I want you. To stay that is." He held his hand out to Wyatt who took hold of it gently.

"We'll give you a minute." Ash dragged Chris out of the room and down to the kitchen where his mom had made up a tray of sandwiches for them all.

"Thanks, Mom." Ash pulled her into a hug, making her squeak in shock.

"Honey, I love all three of you as if you were all my own. I just wish..." she trailed off.

"You wish what?"

"Nothing, honey. You take these up while I get the spare bed made up." She bustled out of the kitchen.

"She was gonna say something about Wes'

mom and dad, wasn't she?" Chris asked, his voice still small.

"Yeah, I think so. Let's take these up."

As they walked up the stairs, Chris stopped suddenly.

"Oh, what did Camille say when you asked her out?"

Shit.

20

Wes slept for almost sixteen hours, leaving Chris and Wyatt to crowd in Ash's room so as not to wake him. They didn't do much, all three of them were, Ash knew, too worried about Wes to do anything or even leave the house.

His mom stuck her head around the door. "Honey, where are Wes' clothes? I'll run them through the wash for him."

"I'll grab them for you." Chris jumped to his feet and slipped into the spare room.

"D'you think I should head over to his house and get him some more?" Ash asked his mom.

"If you want to, or your dad can go over."

"No, I think I should do it."

"Please, watch your tone with them. I don't want you getting into trouble."

"I'm an angel, Mother." He couldn't help but grin when she rolled her eyes before taking the pile of clothes off Chris. "You guys coming with?" he asked Wyatt and Chris; the latter had stuck his head back around the door.

"Do you mind if I stay here? I know things won't go well, and I don't need that right now." Chris said. Ash patted his shoulder, nodding.

"I'll come." Wyatt's voice was hard, and Ash wondered if it was going to be a mistake taking him.

"Sure, let's go."

Wyatt followed him outside as Chris went to sit next to Wes' bed.

"What's Chris' deal? I thought he'd want to come too."

"Normally he would, but he doesn't do well with arguments thanks to his dad's shitty temper. He'd much rather avoid them as much as he can, and I won't force him to be there when I give Wes' dad some home truths."

"Am I gonna need bail money?"

"Not gonna lie, I don't know."

Although it wasn't far to Wes' house, Ash

drove because he wasn't sure how much stuff they were going to bring back with them. When he pulled up outside the house, he noticed the family car wasn't on the drive.

"Maybe they're not home," he commented as he and Wyatt approached the front door.

"You sound almost disappointed about that." Wyatt laughed, a wry sound nothing like his usual laugh.

"Yeah, I think I am." He knocked on the door. When no one answered, rather than get back into his car, Ash went around the side of the house, climbed over the gate and into the back yard.

"What are you doing?"

"I'm getting Wes' stuff." Ash started climbing the drainpipe which he knew led directly to Wes' bedroom window. It was open a crack, enough for him to slide his hand through and push it open further. "Go round to the front door, I'll let you in." He called down to Wyatt before slipping into a bedroom he knew almost as well as his own.

Without stopping, he made his way downstairs to let Wyatt inside and they went back up to Wes' room. He pulled Wes' backpack out of his closet and began shoving clothes into it, not caring that he was making a bit of a mess. Over his shoulder, he asked Wyatt to grab toiletries from the bathroom Wes shared with his sister. At the thought of Lizzie, Ash snuck into her bedroom, grabbed a sheet of paper, and left a note for her on her desk.

Wes at my house. Visit whenever you want. Ash.

Once they had what they needed, Ash led the way downstairs without a care in the world. As he reached out to open the front door, it opened from the outside and Wes' dad walked in, a mixture of surprise and annoyance on his face.

"Ash? What are you doing in the house?"

"Wes gave me his key. He needed some clean clothes, and you know, he's not able to come and get them himself due to the cracked rib he got when he was attacked." He didn't even bother keeping the spite from his voice, not when all he wanted to do was punch the man.

"Oh... right. Er..."

"He's not okay, but he will be. Thanks to my mom and dad."

"Come on, dude." Ash looked at Wyatt

nodding toward the front door. They left without saying goodbye and walked to Ash's car.

"Dude, you're shaking. Are you gonna be okay?"

"I will be, but just give me a minute and don't let me turn back and hit him."

Ash hated the fact Wes' parents, his dad especially, didn't accept him for who he was. Didn't realize he was still their son. He hated how Wes had to walk on eggshells around them. Only Lizzie was a light in his life at home, something Ash would never be able to thank her for enough.

Eventually, he calmed down enough to unlock his car, shoving Wes' stuff onto the back seat.

"Thanks for being here. I don't think my mom would appreciate having to pick me up from the police station." They climbed into the car and Ash started the engine.

"Can I ask you something?" Wyatt asked as Ash drove away from the house they'd just broken into.

"Sure, bro. Anything."

"What happened between you and Wes?"

:: ::

Back at home and with Wyatt okay with his and Wes' past, Ash sat on his bed with his journal. Trying to channel his anger into some semblance of lyrics was proving difficult and it was frustrating the hell out of him.

"I'm going for a drive, you guys gonna be okay for a while?" Chris was still at his house, lounging on the airbed. Wyatt was splitting his time between the room Wes was sleeping in and Ash's room. Ash thought he looked uncomfortable, but knew he stayed because he was worried about the boy in the bed in the next room. The boy he was clearly growing to care about a lot.

"Sure, you go ahead." Chris dismissed him with a brief wave as he kept his eyes locked on his phone.

Heading downstairs, he managed to get outside without either of his parents stopping and questioning him. Taking his car out of park, he let it roll out of the drive and onto the road before starting the engine and pulling away. Once he was far enough away from his house, he turned on the radio and cranked up the volume as Nirvana's *Smells Like Teen Spirit* started. As he drove with no destination in mind, the ear-splitting music hammered into his head.

Eventually, he brought the car to a stop and looked out of the window as he turned the volume down to a more acceptable level. He was outside *Downtown Beans* and could see Camille behind the counter through the window. Taking a deep breath, he got out of the car, locked the door, and walked into the coffee house.

"Hey Ash, how's Wes?" Of course she remembered. She was clearly a nice person who cared about people, even those she barely knew.

"He's doing okay. Be a while before he's back on the drums though." He ordered a coffee and sat down at a table wondering to himself why he was there. As it was quiet, Camille snuck out from behind the counter and sat down with him.

"Did the guys get caught?" She asked after he'd told her what had happened.

"One of them, but we don't know what's going on. My dad's been in contact with the police because Wes is staying with us."

"Why isn't he with his family?"

Ash explained about how his parents hated the fact they had a gay son and how most of the time, Wes had to pretend to be 'normal' whenever he was at home.

"I don't know if this attack will change things between them or not. But Wes knows he has family in me and Chris. He knows we love him no matter what, and my house is a safe space for him."

Camille put her hand on top of his, the one that was tapping the table-top almost violently.

"I'm glad he has you both. No one should feel they have to hide who they are just to please someone else."

All Ash could think about was how small her hand felt compared to his, how warm and smooth her skin was. Slowly, he turned his own hand over and linked his long fingers through hers.

"Go out with me tomorrow." He didn't exactly ask, but he needed to say it. He looked into her brown eyes, hoping she would say yes.

"Okay."

21

Ash stood in his bedroom, a towel wrapped around his waist and his hair dripping from his shower.

"Guys, I don't know what to wear on a date." Chris and Wes were squashed together on his bed, leaning up against his headboard. Wes was looking a lot better, but still winced too much for Ash's liking. When he'd slept through the pain meds the doctor had given him, he'd sent Wyatt home to catch up with some sleep. The surfer had missed three days of work at the surf store and he'd had to turn his phone off to stop the messages from his boss coming through. He hadn't wanted to leave, but Wes forced him with a kiss and a promise that once he was up to it, Wyatt could take him surfing.

"Clothes would be a good start." Wes deadpanned, making Chris snort.

"You're lucky you're hurt, and I can't hit you right now."

"Stop freaking out. Remember the shirt you wore to graduation? Wear that, with some black jeans, and boots, not sneakers."

"I really could make a comment about you being the stereotypical gay best friend, but I'm far too grateful to be that crass."

Wes laughed, wincing, as Ash rummaged through his closet, getting out the clothes Wes had ordered him to wear.

"Hey, Ash. Wanna borrow my leather?" Chris asked.

"Thanks, but it's cool. I'll stick with my shirt." He leaned over to fist bump his friend.

"Where are you taking her anyway?" Wes asked. Ash had kept quiet about his plans for the date with Camille, not because he was nervous, but because he was worried they'd think it was lame.

"We're going to the beach. I've got a picnic in the trunk of my car. Mom helped me pack it."

"Dude, I didn't know you were so romantic." Chris fluttered his eyelashes at Ash who was buttoning up his shirt, leaving the top two undone.

"Stop teasing him. She'll love it." Wes smiled at Ash, which helped ease the grip his nerves had on him as he went into the bathroom to try to tame his shaggy hair. Giving up, he pulled on a black beanie. Once he was ready, he checked he had everything he needed. When he was satisfied he was as ready as he was going to be, he left the guys watching his TV and went downstairs.

"Honey, you look so handsome, but the hat..."

He laughed at his mom before placing a kiss on her cheek.

"I'll see you later." Swiping his keys off the end table in the living room, he made his way outside. As he reached his car, he spotted a petite blonde hovering on the sidewalk. "Lizzie, that you?"

Wes' sister jumped at the sound of her name.

"Hi. I was wondering if I could go in and see him?" Ash wrapped her up in a hug.

"Of course you can. Come on, I'll let you in." He walked the girl into the house, and introduced her to his mom and dad, before taking her upstairs.

"Wes, you got a visitor."

Lizzie stepped out from behind him. "Hey, big brother."

Sneaking away, he finally managed to get on his way to pick Camille up.

:: ::

As they sat on the beach, Ash couldn't stop thinking how beautiful Camille looked. It wasn't anything to do with the clothes she wore or the minimal make-up she had on, but there was something about the way the sunset lit up her skin and made her hair glow.

"This food is delicious. Where did you buy it from?" she asked, picking up some more of the salad he and his mom had prepared earlier in the day.

"I'll have you know I made it all."

She looked at him, impressed and he wanted her to always have that look on her face.

"Admittedly, my mom helped, but I did most of it."

"Wow. A great musician and he can cook."

"Clearly I'm layered."

"Clearly." Looking away, Camille put some of the chicken he'd cooked into her mouth and Ash found himself unable to look away from her lips. Not for the first time since he'd picked her up outside her dorm, he wanted to kiss her. "It really is beautiful here. I haven't been to the beach in forever."

"Me neither if I'm honest. I'm always too busy with music."

"It shows. You know how to put on a show. You've got stage presence that should be illegal in someone your age."

"Thanks?" They both laughed as the conversation between them stilled. Ash looked out over the ocean, savoring the breeze washing over him. It was warm and being so close to Camille had upped his body temperature a few degrees.

"It was a compliment." She dropped the tomato she was holding back into the tub. "My god, I'm stuffed."

"How about we put this lot back in the trunk of my car and go for a walk?" Ash suggested.

"That sounds great. You can tell me how you and your boys met."

They packed away the picnic, Camille

shaking out the sand from the blanket before folding it, then they walked together back to Ash's car. Once everything was safely back in the trunk of his car, they made their way back onto the sand and began walking toward the pier as Ash told her all about meeting his best friends.

"Chris literally body slammed me in the hallway in elementary trying to get away from a toy spider another kid was chasing him with. Not been able to shake him off ever since."

"And you wouldn't want to." She laughed.

"I really wouldn't. I can't imagine not having that dork in my life." They both laughed and Ash felt his arm heat up when Camille's brushed up against it. He'd rolled his shirt sleeves up, and her skin was warm from the setting sun.

"What about Wes? How did you meet him?"

"He transferred to our middle school in like sixth grade. A teacher sat him next to Chris to try and offset the 'new kid nerves' during one of their classes, and then Chris spilled his milk all over Wes at lunch. We've been friends ever since."

"I bet you three were a nightmare together."

"I'll have you know we were completely adorable." He grinned at her. "Well, I was. Chris' always been a bit..."

"Dubious?"

"Something like that, yeah." His fingers were twitching. Not only to write lyrics about her, but to hold her hand as they walked. "How did you and Leah meet?"

"Her family moved into the house next door when we were six. As her mom unloaded their stuff, she came into the front yard, introduced herself. Been best friends ever since."

Ash tried to picture a six-year-old Camille and couldn't quite conjure up the image.

"That sounds like Leah all right."

As she laughed, Camille stumbled on the sand. Ash managed to grab hold of her hands to prevent her from landing on her ass.

"Thanks," she gasped as they started walking again. It didn't escape Ash's notice that she still held onto one of his hands. There was no way he could wipe the smile off his face now.

:: ::

Ash pulled up outside Camille's dorm. It was almost one am and she had work the next morning. Getting out of the car, he walked around the hood to help her out before walking her to her building.

"Thanks for tonight, it's been great," she told him as they approached the doors.

"It has." Ash could hear voices approaching them from behind, but all of his focus was on the petite girl in front of him, the girl he was desperate to kiss.

"Whoa, Camille. He's hot. Where d'ya find him?" a girl called out as she and her friends passed the couple. Ash chuckled as Camille hid her face in his chest. He wrapped his arms around her and called out.

"Believe me, I'm the lucky one here, girls."

A fresh round of giggles filled the air as Camille groaned in his arms.

"Oh my god, I'm so sorry about that." She sounded embarrassed and tried to pull away from him, still hiding her face. Carefully, he lifted her chin up so he could make eye contact with her.

"Don't be." With a quick glance down at her lips, he bent his head and place a soft kiss on them. "I hope we can do this again."

"Me too." Camille raised herself up onto her tiptoes and initiated another kiss. This one was definitely not chaste, and Ash felt it throughout his entire body.

22

Letting himself into the house, Ash managed to sneak up the stairs to his room without waking his parents or Wes, but when he got into his bedroom, Chris was still sat on Ash's bed, wide awake. It was obvious he had been waiting for him, strumming his unplugged bass.

"Hey, bro, how did it go?" he asked, putting his bass on the stand next to the bed. "Was the picnic a hit?"

"I think so." Ash couldn't stop the smile spreading across his face. Chris just winked at him.

"From the look on your face, I'd say you know more than you're letting on, but I'll wait."

He picked his bass back up and plucked a few strings, a country twang filling Ash's room.

"A gentleman never kisses and tells."

"So, there was a kiss..." Ash ignored the question and threw his beanie, hitting Chris square in the face, making him squeak in surprise.

"Shut up and go to sleep."

He stripped down to his boxers, and slid under the covers, pushing Chris off and onto the airbed beside them.

"Dick."

"Yep."

Waking up in the morning, the first thing that crossed Ash's mind was the feel of Camille's lips against his own and he couldn't stop the way it made him feel. Suddenly remembering Chris was in the room, he climbed out of bed and made his way into the shower to take care of things.

When he emerged, a towel wrapped around his waist, Chris was awake, and Wes had come into Ash's room. The pair of them watched him moving around, matching smirks on their face.

"What?" He tried to not to look at them, but when their sniggering started, he couldn't help it.

"Did you... bro, did you just crack one out in the shower while I was innocently sleeping in here?" Chris asked, making Ash mentally facepalm.

"I was showering. People do that, you know?" He grabbed his fresh clothes and went back into the bathroom to pull them on, needing to be away from his two best friends, especially the ginger one who was watching him, eyebrows raised and a wide, smug smile on his face. He could hear them still cackling as he pulled on his favorite jeans and one of his many band tees. He exited the bathroom, ignoring the two idiots on his bed, before he slid his feet into his sneakers and grabbed his acoustic.

"Are you two staying here today?" he asked as he loaded his journal into his backpack along with some picks and a hoodie.

"Hell, no. We're coming with you. We want to see you being all gooey around Camille." Wes grinned as Chris nodded his head like a bobblehead.

"I really hate you guys."

:: ::

As Ash and Chris set up, Wes went inside *Downtown Beans* and ordered some drinks before taking a seat inside the window where he could watch and listen without causing himself too much pain.

"Camille's working." Chris commented as he secured his mic stand.

"I have eyes, Chris. I can see her."

"Aren't you going to say hi before we start?"

"She's busy, and so am I. I'm sure I can chat to her later. Now, what are we starting with, and no, *Cowboy Blues* is not an option." Chris pouted as Ash began the intro to his favorite Green Day track. *Wake Me Up When September Ends* was such a meaningful song and as a songwriter, Ash couldn't help but fall in love with the story the song told and how personal it was without being cloying.

Wes had come out and recorded a few videos of the two of them, and by the time they'd finished and had packed away their gear, he'd posted the clips to Instagram. They were amassing likes and comments – mostly, to the amusement of Chris – about Ash's looks which still frustrated him. Why couldn't the comments be about the music over how attractive he looked in his beanie?

They sat inside *Downtown Beans* and

ordered some food so Wes could take a fresh round of pain meds before Ash took him back to the house as ordered by his mom. She was so worried about Wes, as they all were, and had stepped up amazingly in place of Wes' own parents.

"Hey, how did it go with Lizzie last night?" he asked as they sat around their table. He'd almost forgotten about her visit in the euphoria left over from his date with Camille.

"Really good. She's trying to make plans for when she can move out so we can get an apartment together." He smiled at the thought, but Ash wondered if it would ever happen now that Wyatt was on the scene.

"Did you tell her about Wyatt?" Chris asked, even though he'd been at the house when Ash had gone out. "I left them alone for privacy." He explained, clearing that bit of confusion up for him. Wes had been holding back from his sister about Wyatt as he didn't know how serious things would get, but it was clear things had changed after the attack.

"I did. She thinks he sounds cute and can't wait to meet him."

"He's a cool dude. I really like him, and after

the last few days, I have mad respect for him," Ash told his ex. It didn't feel weird for him to be discussing his ex's current boyfriend; they were friends first and always would be.

"I'm glad. I don't think I could have coped if you didn't like him, either of you." Wes winced as he swallowed his meds.

"Time to get you home, or my mom will kill all three of us." He handed Chris his car keys, saying he needed to go to the bathroom and would meet them at the car. Judging by the looks on their faces, neither of them believed his white lie.

As he approached the counter where Camille was busy, she caught his eye and smiled brightly at him before mouthing 'give me a second' at him. Smoothly, he watched her and Leah swap positions so she could come out to meet him. As soon as she was close enough, she stood up on her tiptoes to place a gentle kiss on his lips. He was glad she did, as he hadn't been sure how to greet her when he saw her, and it had been plaguing him all morning.

"You sounded great out there today."

"Thanks, I was in a pretty good mood." His confession made her laugh. "Are you busy tonight?" He asked, mentally crossing his fingers behind his back.

"Yeah, I am. It's movie night with Ben and my dad."

"Oh, okay."

"I can be free tomorrow though...?"

"I'll pick you up at six. I hope you like the fair." He bent his head and gave her another quick kiss. Calling out a goodbye to Leah, he forced himself out of the coffee house and out to his car where his friends were waiting for him.

"You look like you're in a good mood," Wes commented.

"I am. Me and Camille are going out again tomorrow night." At his words, Chris slapped some money into Wes' hand. "Were you guys betting on me asking her out again?"

"Of course, and naturally, I won." Rolling his eyes at the smug look on Wes' face, Ash climbed into the car and drove home.

Wes climbed into the bed in the spare room, exhaustion hitting him after doing too much. Chris and Ash sat with him for a while, but when it became clear he was going to be out for a good few hours, they moved into Ash's room.

"You think he'll be okay?" Chris asked, a hint of worry in his voice.

"Yeah, he's tougher than he thinks, but I don't think he'll get over it too quick though. It's really messed with his mind, and I totally get it."

"Is that why you keep your sexuality close to your chest?"

"I guess so, but I don't see it as me doing that. I'm not hiding who I am. I just don't need to advertise it. I guess it would be different if I'd met a guy rather than a girl, but I don't really know."

"You know, until this last week, I never really got it. I mean, I've always known about prejudice out there, but because it never affected me directly, I didn't realize how prolific it still is. Seeing Wes in so much pain because some guys thought they had the right to attack him and Wyatt hurt, man. Now I know why you went off at Joey the way you did. I'm sorry."

"Chris, you have no reason to apologize." Ash wrapped his arm around his friend and pulled him in for a squeeze. "You've got one of the biggest hearts of anyone I know, and just because you didn't understand it, didn't mean you swept it away. I've seen you stand up to idiots at school, so don't ever downplay how much you matter.

187

Even if you are a huge dork." Chris snorted out a laugh.

"I just can't believe people think that way. Who someone else loves has no bearing on my life, so why should it bother anyone?"

"I don't know, bro. I really don't."

Silence fell over them as they both disappeared into their own minds for a while.

"Hey, wanna come over for Ben's lesson this afternoon?" Ash asked.

"Sure."

23

Ash had driven over to Santa Monica so he and Camille could spend time on the pier. They wandered through the crowds, hand in hand, stopping every now and then to share kisses that took his breath away. They hid in dark corners away from prying eyes as things got heated between them, before they came to their senses and remerged into the crowds, playing the games and going on rides.

Ash hadn't felt like a kid in a long time, but right there and then, he could forget about the crap with Wes, the problems Chris had with his family, and just enjoy himself. There was something about Camille that made him want to live in the moment rather than constantly looking to the future.

"Are you hungry?" he asked her as he handed her a soft toy he'd won. It was a bright purple butterfly, and she was hugging it tightly.

"I could eat."

"Do you want to eat here, or head closer to home?"

"Let's head closer to home. There's a great burrito place near campus."

"Sold." Taking hold of her hand once more, they walked back to where he'd parked his car. Before they got in, Ash backed Camille up against it, caging her in his arms which rested on the roof either side of her, before kissing her deeply. She tasted like cotton candy and the mint of the gum she'd been chewing earlier in the evening and he couldn't get enough.

Breathless, he pulled away and locked eyes with her. He could see her struggling to control her own breathing.

"Hi." He felt like an idiot for saying it, but it was all his brain could muster up in the moment.

"Hey."

The pair of them stood like that for a while,

until Camille's stomach rumbled. Ash actually snorted at the sound.

"Come on, let's go and get some food."

:: ::

After dropping Camille off at her dorm, Ash went home. Wes was asleep, with Wyatt curled up next to him, but Chris was nowhere to be seen. Assuming he'd gone home for a while, Ash climbed into his bed, but was unable to sleep. Sitting up, he grabbed his journal off the night-stand and opened to a fresh page.

Picturing Camille under the lights from the rides on the pier, Ash began to scribble down his thoughts. They weren't exactly lyrics, but it felt like he *needed* to get the words down on paper before he got a migraine from them whirling around in his mind. Once he'd finished, he'd filled almost three pages of words and phrases. Unable to make any cohesive sense of them at almost four am, he put the journal down and tried to get some sleep but was too wired.

Eventually, giving up, he climbed out of bed, pulled some sweats on, and went downstairs. In the kitchen, he made himself a drink and pulled a bag of chips out of the cupboard. He sat on the work top, eating his way through the bag, scrolling through his social media.

Camille had tagged him in an Instagram post, a selfie they'd taken on the Ferris wheel at the pier. In the photo, he was looking at her rather than at the camera and he didn't recognize the look on his own face. It was soft and relaxed, and it was all her fault.

A great night was had thanks to this gorgeous hunk of a dork.

The fact she'd called him gorgeous publicly, and a hunk, sent shivers of excitement down his spine. Then he read the comments.

OMG! He's so cute, where do I find one?

Gurrrrl! I gotta get me one of these.

Cam, the way he's looking at you tho.

Damn, girl. You got yourself a snack!

Laughing to himself, Ash came out of the comments before scrolling further through his feed. He didn't have a personal account, just the band one, which Camille had tagged in the photo. Thanks to that, a few more people had followed the band, and the video clips Wes had posted were getting even more likes and comments.

Things needed to move faster though. They needed to book a showcase somewhere so they could get the attention of industry people. Rare Breed could be huge, they just needed the right person to hear their music.

While Wes was recovering, rehearsals were out of the question, so Ash decided to start looking at venues to book some shows. Once he got some sleep that is.

:: ::

Ash's dad took Wes back to the hospital to get him checked over to make sure his recovery was going well. Ash had wanted to go with them, but as they were going to Wes' house after, he thought it was best he stayed away. He was still full of rage at Wes' parents for abandoning their son the way they had, and his dad was better suited to deal with any tension than Ash ever would be.

Chris was at school and it was raining, so Ash couldn't go and play outside *Downtown Beans,* but he could go and sit inside with his laptop and make a start on trying to find more shows for Rare Breed. He shoved the machine into his backpack along with his journal before grabbing a jacket and running out to his car.

When he arrived, the coffee house was almost empty. Leah and Brian were behind the counter doing what looked like some kind of inventory, so Ash waited to be served rather than interrupt them. Eventually, Leah spotted him and hustled to get him his order.

"Well, music man, I gotta say you and my girl make a mighty fine-looking couple. I'm impressed." She held her phone up, the photo Camille had posted of them on the screen.

Laughing, Ash took a small bow. When he straightened up, he noticed Brian glaring at him. Flashing the guy a smile, he dug out some cash for his coffee and muffin, plus a tip for Leah.

"I guess I have you to thank for giving me the push to ask her out, so thanks."

Leah turned to Brian and muttered, "I'm taking my break," and she came around the counter to join Ash at his table.

"Are you gonna give me the best friend speech?" he asked, feeling the corner of his mouth lift in a smile.

"No, because if you hurt her, it's not me you

gotta look out for. It's her. I'll just be her back-up."

Feeling somewhat nervous, Ash tried to laugh her words off, but didn't quite manage it.

"Right, I'll keep that in mind."

"So, what brings you here when the gorgeous Ms. Rogers isn't?"

Ash explained about Wes and his dad being out and how he was using the unexpected spare time to scout shows.

"Try The Vine over in West Hollywood. They do a couple showcase events for unsigned acts a month. It's a new place and the guy who owns it has links with The Troubadour and a few other big name venues. If you can get in there, you can get into any of the main venues in the city." Ash flashed her a grateful smile, opened his browser, then stopped. "Oh, the Wi-Fi password is 'beans', but I'm not supposed to tell you that."

Ash leaned over and gave the girl a kiss on the cheek.

"Are you keeping track of all these favors I owe you?"

"I wiped it clean when you made Camille happy. Just please, treat her right."

"I promise." With a smile, Leah left him to do

his research and went back to work. As he watched her walk away, he once again noticed the dirty looks Brian was giving him. With a shrug, he turned his attention to the screen on his laptop.

The next time he looked up, stretching out his back, there were a few more customers around him, and his coffee was stone cold. He pulled his phone out of his pocket to check the time. It was almost four, so he knew his dad and Wes would be back, so rather than order another drink, he put all his stuff away and took his half empty cup and plate over to the counter. Leah wasn't anywhere to be seen and Brian ignored him as he placed both items on the counter.

With a cheery smile and a snarky 'have a nice day', Ash turned his back on Brian and walked toward the door.

"Hey, you." Brian's voice called out. Ash smirked to himself as he turned to face the guy. "You're no good for her, you know? Why don't you do the best thing and forget about her?"

"So you can slither in to comfort her? It's okay, I think I'll leave the choices up to Camille." Lifting his hand in a mock salute, Ash left the coffee shop and ran through the rain to his car.

24

Wes sat at Ash's desk catching up with the homework Chris had been collecting for him.

"How did it go?" Ash asked as he entered his bedroom.

"I'm healing nicely. Another week off school, just to be sure I don't knock it or anything. As for the drums, after next week I can play, but nothing too heavy or for too long."

"That's awesome, bro. What about the other thing?"

"It could have been worse, but it could have been better too. Mom was okay, worried about me, but Dad... well, you know what he can be like."

"Yeah, I do."

"Well, your dad asked them if it was still okay for me to stay here, and it's all cool with them. I never really expected them to refuse. It means I'm out of their hair, and they don't need to pretend I'm not there. I managed to grab some more clothes, my laptop, and my spare sticks. Beyond that, I don't need much else." He was smiling, but Ash knew him well enough to tell he was hurt by his parents' rejection. Kneeling in front of the chair, he managed to wrap his arms around Wes, gently hugging him.

"I know you guys were a thing way back when, but have I missed something?" Chris' voice made them both jump as he climbed in through the window.

"Dude, it's still daylight, why aren't you using the door?" Ash asked as he climbed to his feet, somehow keeping hold of Wes' hand.

"Habit, I guess." He jumped into the room and gave Wes a fist bump. "So, why are we hugging, and do I need to get in on the action?"

"Wes had a shitty day and needed cheering up." Ash felt that was the simplest answer, for now.

While Chris and Wes did homework, Ash

continued to research places they could try to get showcases. As he was reading about a venue, his phone buzzed. Looking at the screen, he saw a message from Camille.

Hey, are you guys busy tomorrow?

Guys, as in multiple? *wink wink*

Very funny. The band. I have some possible news. Meet me at my dad's place around five?

We'll be there.

"Boys, something's happening tomorrow and we gotta go over to the studio."

"What is it?" Typical Wes, needing more detail before committing to anything.

"I have no clue, but we'll find out tomorrow."

At that moment, Ash's mom called them down for food, and when they reached the kitchen, Wyatt was already sat down, a plate in front of him and a bewildered look on his face.

:: ::

With everything that had happened, it felt as if it had been ages since Ash had been to the studio. As the four of them walked inside he took a deep breath, loving the smell of the space around him. Wood, a hint of paint, and something he could never quite identify relaxed him. There was also the hint of sweaty musicians, but he managed to ignore that a little.

"I've missed coming in here," Wes told Wyatt as he moved to sit behind his drumkit, the band logo standing out from the bass drum. Ash watched as he ran his hands over the skins and cymbals, clearly itching to wail on them, but unable to. Wyatt stood behind him, draping his arms over Wes' shoulder, clutching at his boyfriend's hands. Turning away to give them privacy, he watched as Chris flopped onto the couch and closed his eyes.

"You okay, man?"

"I'm good. Just savoring the quiet. There's too much noise lately, and it's getting to me."

Worried, Ash walked over to the couch and sat down next to him.

"Talk to me."

"Just the usual, you know?" Ash did know. Whenever Chris stayed at home, the fighting kept him awake until the early hours of the morning. His eyes would have deep, black circles under them for days, but still, his friend tried to spend as much time at home as possible. It was always easier for his mom when he did, and Ash knew the guilt at needing time away ate into him.

"Yeah, I know, bro."

The two of them stayed on the couch. The only sound was the murmuring of Wyatt and Wes having a quiet conversation.

Chris was fast asleep, his head lolled on Ash's shoulder, and Ash was dozing when Camille and Leah slid the doors open and stepped inside.

"Well, this all looks cozy." Leah commented, one of her eyebrows raised as she took in Ash and Chris. The bassist was still asleep, so Ash managed to slide out from under him without waking him.

"Sssh. He doesn't get much sleep, leave him to it."

Leah's face softened at his words as Camille pulled a blanket out of a closet and draped it over the sleeping boy before making her way over to stand next to Ash. Their hands joined, fingers entwined, and Ash couldn't help but lean into her slightly. The coffee smell in her hair was missing, replaced by the subtle aroma of coconut.

"Okay. I spoke to one of my professors at school who has contacts all over Hollywood, and he's given me the heads up. The Vine, that new club I told you about, is definitely looking for unsigned acts to perform showcases for industry types and I think you guys should sign up.'" Quiet whooping occurred so Chris wasn't disturbed. Ash and Wes could fill him in later. "The first opening is in two months, and my professor said if you have a demo or anything, he can get you on the list. There's no guarantee, but it's worth a try."

Ash let go of Camille's hand and flung his arms around Leah, who wasn't much shorter than he was, squeezing her tightly. Wes was smiling from behind the drumkit, but didn't move to join in.

"This is amazing, Leah. How long have we got to work on a demo?"

"That's the problem. He kind of needs it by tomorrow. Do you have anything ready?"

"Nothing good enough, no." Wes' entire body shrank back in disappointment.

"Well, we expected this," Camille finally joined the conversation. "And we have a plan." Smiling coyly, she went over to the door and stuck her head through the gap. When she returned, her brother came in behind her, holding a professional looking video camera. "Ben is in his AV Club at school and for extra credit he's been given a challenge to create a short video, no longer than four minutes, that he can showcase at school. Why not cover both bases by getting him to record you guys performing, give it to the guy at The Vine as a demo, and then Ben can use it for school?"

"That is actually genius," Wes blurted out, loudly. Chris suddenly sat bolt upright, mumbling about spiders on ice skates, making Ben laugh.

"I say we have about three hours before it starts getting dark." Ash grinned at everyone in the studio as he grabbed his guitar, plugging it into the amp. He looked at Wes, knowing he shouldn't be drumming, but his friend merely shrugged and grinned at him before beating out a familiar rhythm.

25

"Wes, you need to stop and rest for the rest of the night," Ash told the drummer, seeing him wince more often the longer they rehearsed. "Come on, I'll take you home." He put his guitar back on the stand and waited for Wes to step around the drum kit. "Here, take my keys and I'll meet you in the car." As Wes walked out, Ash turned to Camille who had been watching their rehearsals again.

Ever since their video demo had been accepted by Gabriel West at The Vine almost three days previously, they'd been given a date six weeks away for their showcase. They would be singing no more than four songs, and there would be at least three other acts on the bill, but it was a step in the right direction as far as Ash was concerned. There was no guarantee anyone important would show, but seeing as they were in Los Angeles, anything was a possibility.

"Hey," he spoke softly as she looked up at him, her eyes bright after their high-octane rehearsal. He bent his head to give her a soft kiss, smiling against her lips when she stretched her arms up around his neck.

"Hi," Camille finally spoke when she broke their kiss. "You guys heading back now?"

"I don't have to. I can come back if you want me to?" He hoped she did because he wasn't in the mood to sit at home, even if his best friends were going to be with him.

"That would be great." Camille kissed him again, not so softly this time and Ash struggled to remember he had Wes and Chris waiting in his car for him.

"Give me like, twenty minutes. I'll come right back. I won't even have a shower." The sheen of sweat that covered him from head to toe was cooling even if the rest of him was heating up.

"Is it wrong when I say I'm glad about that?"

Ash laughed, gave her another quick kiss, then bolted out of the garage. The sooner he dropped his friends off, the sooner he could be back with Camille. There had been a promise in her voice he was hoping she'd deliver on.

"Can we pick Wyatt up on the way?" Wes asked as he climbed into the car.

"Sure, man. Chris, where you at tonight?"

"Home, Parker." Chris was in a good mood, so Ash was surprised to hear his friend was going home. He obviously saw a look on Ash's face as he spoke again. "Mom and Dad are away for the weekend and I have the house to myself. I'm gonna make the most of it."

Ash and Wes grinned at him as Ash drove away from the Rogers' house.

:: ::

It was closer to an hour before he pulled his car back into Mr. Rogers' driveway and Ash was starting to freak out. What if Camille was pissed and had left? Yeah, he could have texted her to double check, but in his haste it never even occurred to him.

"Camille? You still here?" He slid the doors to the garage open, but the space was empty. The lights were low, and a bunch of candles had been lit. Music was playing softly in the background which meant she had to be somewhere, he just couldn't see her.

Closing the doors behind him, Ash moved further into the garage and still couldn't see her. Worried she'd left, he walked over to sit on the couch. There, amongst a pile of blankets, was Camille. Fast asleep. With a soft chuckle, he pulled one of the blankets over her, placed a kiss against the wild hair he loved, and went out to the bathroom in the back to wash the now dried sweat from his face and neck. Realizing he needed more, he pulled his shirt off and ran a washcloth over his torso, freshening his skin.

Once he was done, he went out to grab a clean shirt and stopped dead. Camille was awake and staring at him, causing his bare skin to heat up.

"Sorry I took so long," was all he could think of to say.

"Sorry I fell asleep," Camille spoke at the same time.

"If you need to go home to bed, I can drive you over to the dorms."

"I'm fine." Standing up, Camille walked over to him and wrapped her arms around his waist, her hands warm against his bare skin, but the contact still caused him to shiver. "I'd rather stay here."

Ash couldn't prevent the shock of her placing a kiss against his exposed chest from making him jump.

"Why are you so nervous?" she asked, a hint of laughter in her voice.

"Honestly? I don't know." Another kiss, this time on his collarbone, made him groan as he lifted his hands to rest on her waist. Camille stood up on her tiptoes to place a kiss on his lips. What started out as soft and sweet kiss soon turned into much more.

"Lock the door, I kinda don't want my dad or brother stumbling in and interrupting us." Ash was over at the door, sliding the bolt into place in an instant. With a smile on his face, he turned back to look at Camille, who was unbuttoning her shirt. Walking slowly as she removed her top, he took into the glorious sight of her in just her bra. When he was right in front of her, neither of them could hold back anymore, and they fell back onto the couch in a clash of lips and tongues, and a tangle of limbs and discarded clothing.

It was everything Ash had hoped it would be and more.

:: ::

Lying on a pull-out couch in a garage wouldn't usually be Ash's idea of an ideal date but doing all that with Camille curled in against him and soft music playing in the background made it all the better. He stroked a hand across the soft skin on her back as she snuggled in closer to him, a sigh escaping her. He hoped it was one of satisfaction and happiness, because they were the two overwhelming emotions he was feeling.

"If I ask you a question, will you be honest with me?" she asked, sounding sleepy.

"I'll always be honest with you, Camille." He placed a kiss against her forehead, tasting a hint of salt, from the sweat that had built up there earlier.

"The way you hover around Wes... I mean, all three of you guys are crazy close, which is great, but you seem extra protective of him..."

"That's not a question." He'd wondered when this conversation would happen. He just hadn't expected to happen just after sex.

"Is there a specific reason you're like that with him?"

Pulling himself into a seated position, Ash wrapped his arms around himself, suddenly very nervous about how she would react. He really didn't want her to look at him as if he were dirty somehow. Especially not after what they'd just experienced together. Would she now regret what they'd done?

"We've always been close, the three of us, but yeah. There's more to it with me and Wes." Ash couldn't look her in the face, couldn't keep eye contact with her. If what he was about to say was going disgust her, he'd rather not see it and be able to remember her looking at him as if he were someone she could love. "We were together, as a couple for a while. It didn't last long because we realized we were better off as friends, but he meant a lot to me. He still does and it's been almost a year."

Silence fell over them as Camille considered what he'd told her. The longer it lasted, the more Ash wanted to pull his clothes on and leave. He hated feeling as if she was judging him for something that happened before she knew him, and he was ready to explode when she finally spoke.

"Thank you for telling me." She placed her hand on his jaw, turning his head so she could look him in the eyes. "I think it's wonderful you care so much about him, and thank you for trusting me enough to tell me. I know it couldn't have been easy." She placed a gentle kiss on his lips. Once again, it soon turned deeper and more intense.

The last thought that flittered through Ash's mind as he took her naked body into his arms was that he loved her.

26

"**W**e're gonna be late," Wes grumbled from the back seat of Ash's car. It didn't help with Ash's bad mood. They'd been called out of rehearsals by Gabriel West for a meeting at The Vine and it had pissed Ash off because he'd wanted to get over to *Downtown Beans* to set up for a couple of hours until Camille finished work.

"You can get out and walk if you're that fucking worried," he snapped. Instantly, his anger fizzled away and he looked at Wes in his rearview mirror. "I'm sorry, man."

Wes squeezed his shoulder, muttering, "Don't worry about it, bro."

Eventually, Ash managed to park up and the

three of them ran inside. Not as late as they'd been worried they would be, but still late nonetheless.

"Boys, my meetings begin on time." Gabriel West was huge. Not only was he tall, he was broad and imposing, and Ash bit down his retort as they all sat down in his huge office.

"Sorry, won't happen again," Wes tried to placate him.

"See that it doesn't. Now, I've been going through the details for your show and I have a few things I need to discuss with you. First up is the matter of payment." Chris tapped Ash's thigh in excitement at the word. "You have two ways of doing this. You can either pay me the fee or earn it via ticket sales."

"Excuse me, Mr. West. I'm not sure I understand here. We pay you to perform at the showcase?" Ash found his voice.

"Of course. Each act is given a set amount of tickets to sell to cover their performance fee. For any tickets sold after those, you earn two dollars out of every ten of the ticket face value." He looked at the three of them, a smirk on his face. "You didn't think this was going to be free, did you?"

"Well..." Wes drew out the word, his voice pitched higher than it usually was.

"Look, boys. This is my business, and the point of a business is to make a profit. I give up-and-comers not unlike yourselves a chance to perform in front of the cream of the music biz crop, but I need to make a profit after covering my overheads."

"How many tickets do we need to sell?" Ash asked, feeling dejected. He was mentally kicking himself for not researching all this properly.

"One hundred. At ten bucks a piece." Chris almost fell off his seat.

"That's like, a grand," he squeaked.

"Well done, you know your math. I'll leave the decision in your hands, but I need to know by the end of this week which way you're going to pay. Once that's decided, I suggest you begin promoting the showcase as much as you can to sell those tickets."

"Yes, sir," Ash said and the three of them stood up. "Thank you for the opportunity."

"Nice to meet you, boys. Speak soon."

They were dismissed.

:: ::

"I can't believe we were so fucking naïve. I really want to go and tell Gabriel fucking West to shove his showcase up his ass, but I can't do that. Not now. We're so close to making it, I can almost taste it."

Ash was pacing back and forth in the garage with Camille watching, chewing on her thumbnail. Chris and Wes had gone to meet up with Wyatt and to bring back food.

"When do you get the tickets?" she asked, trying to calm him down.

"I have no idea. We've got until the end of the week to decide what we're doing."

"Ash, sit down. You're giving me motion sickness." She yanked on his arm, pulling him onto the couch next to her. "Look, there are six weeks until the showcase. That's plenty of time for us to get promoting. The tickets will sell like crazy because you guys are so good. People will be fighting over them."

"I'm glad someone has faith."

"*You* need to have faith, or this entire thing is gonna end up being a non-starter."

As she spoke, Ash let out a huge sigh just as Chris and Wes walked in.

"Have you calmed him down yet?" Wes

asked, placing a couple pizza boxes on the small table in front of the couch.

"I'm calm. Camille's right. We need to make our decision and promote the hell out of this show. Even if we don't make any money, we need the attention it can bring us."

"How do we do that?" Chris asked. Camille had her phone in her hand and was tapping away at the screen.

"We use our secret weapon," she told them.

"Huh?" All three members of Rare Breed were confused, making Camille laugh.

"We have a Leah. She's on her way. Now someone pass me a slice. I'm starved."

:: ::

Within ten minutes of Leah arriving, she not only had access to the Rare Breed social media accounts, but she'd already mocked up a poster for the show on her laptop.

"You're... you... how do you do this shit so fast?" Ash asked as she played around with colors and added a few more details to the poster.

"This is the kind of stuff I want to be doing,

so think of me as an intern. Just pay me in tickets and pizza."

All three guys piled onto the couch to give her hugs. It was the only way any of them could think of to express their gratitude. Seeing Camille laughing at them, Ash grabbed hold of her and pulled her into their pile. As the others remained hugging Leah, Ash couldn't resist kissing Camille, shutting their friends out for a moment.

The moment ended when Chris and Wes shoved the pair of them off the couch. Wes didn't even wince, that much, a sign he was almost back to full health.

"I won't print these out until you've spoken to Gabriel, but they're ready to go and I know a print shop that will do me a deal," Leah told them once everyone had begun to calm down.

"Let me know how much so I can get you the cash out of the band fund," Ash told her. "I'll even come with you to pick them up."

"Just give me the go ahead and I'll start setting everything up online. I will get you guys a full house."

"Leah, you're the absolute best." Chris held his hand out for a high five, which she gave him with passion, making him shake out his hand after the contact.

"You know it. Now, let me eat in peace. My work here is done, for now."

The five of them descended into a comfortable silence as they ate. Eventually, it was time for them all to leave. Wes was staying over at Wyatt's – after promising Ash's mom he had his last few pain meds with him – and Chris was still at his own house. For the first time in what felt like forever, Ash would be all alone in his bedroom, and he wasn't sure how he felt about it. As they walked out to his and Leah's cars, he pulled Camille in close.

"Hey, wanna have a sleepover?" He felt like a complete dork for phrasing it that way, but it made Camille laugh, and that made everything okay.

"Where, here again?" Her shy smile did things to him he didn't want to happen in public.

"No, my place."

"But what about your parents?"

"What about them?" Ash bit at his lip, worried she was going to refuse. "We'll just have to be quiet."

That made her laugh. "Let me go back to the

dorms and grab some clothes. I'll get Leah to take me."

"I'll pick you up after I drop these two idiots off." He planted a kiss against her lips, and they followed their friends outside.

:: ::

Sneaking Camille into the house and up to his room was easier than Ash had expected, and they were soon lying on his bed, making out as if the world was ending. It didn't take long for their kissing to become more heated as they stripped off, and after Ash made sure his door was locked it didn't take long for their bodies to tangle together as the heat around them rose.

27

The posters for the showcase were everywhere. Leah had filled the band's social media with information about it. She'd even set up a competition for someone to win two free tickets by going into *Downtown Beans* and signing up for a loyalty card. By the end of the first week, they had almost thirty people entered. None of the guys could quite believe what was happening. Not only did people start following their socials, they seemed genuinely interested in their music rather than in Ash's arms and shoulders.

Leah often livestreamed their rehearsals in the garage which all three of them loved because it forced them to work to the best of their capabilities without messing around. It often felt as if they were giving mini gigs from the comfort of their own space.

"Leah's a damn genius, boys," Ash said to Wes and Chris as they sprawled out on his bed, with Wyatt sat on the floor. "At this rate, the showcase will be sold out with loads of time to spare." The idea of playing to a packed-out crowd in a legitimate music venue, even if it was one that belonged to Gabriel West, was intoxicating. The more dealings they had with him in the run up to the showcase, the more Ash actively disliked him.

"She really is. I just hope Gabriel doesn't manage to screw it all up for us somehow," Wes commented, making it clear he didn't like or trust the club owner either.

"Look, if we pack out that room and there ends up being execs and stuff, then I don't care if we never have to deal with Gabriel West ever again." Ash looked up at the ceiling. "It's finally happening for us, boys. Our time to shine is nigh, and we're gonna be legends."

"As long as you legends don't forget about me," Wyatt piped up from where he was sat leaning up against Wes' legs.

"Like we could ever." Wes gently ran his hand through Wyatt's long hair, a soft expression on his face.

"Wyatt, if we make it, you're coming with us, man." Chris held out his hand for a high-five that came from an awkward angle. "What about Camille?" he asked Ash, looking over.

"What about Camille?" Ash was confused by Chris's question.

"Will you invite her on tour with us? If one happens, that is?"

"No. Not because I don't want her there, but because she's at college. She has her own dreams to chase and I could never ask her to put those on hold to support mine."

"Dude, you sound like you've been together for years rather than a few weeks," Wyatt snorted, causing Wes to thump his shoulder without putting any real effort into it.

"It feels like it sometimes. She gets me, the music, everything. Although she wants something different, she still understands the draw."

"He's got his Camille face on again." Chris laughed, dodging the slap Ash tried to land on his thigh. Angling his head better, Ash looked up at Chris who was pulling a soppy face.

"That's not my face." With a shove, Chris rolled off the bed, making the rest of them laugh.

"It's a face."

Ash's mom popped her head around the door and spoke sternly despite the smile on her face, "Boys, any chance you can keep it down or I'll be forced to separate you."

"Sorry, Mrs. Kane."

"Sorry, Mom. We'll shut up now."

Wes and Wyatt stood up and Ash saw that his ex didn't wince when he stretched and yawned. He was pleased for both Wes and the band. The two of them left Ash's room and made their way into the spare room hand-in-hand.

"How come your mom and dad are okay with Wyatt staying over, but you had to sneak Camille in?"

"Because Wes has been hurt, so it's not like they've been able to get up to anything other than making out."

"That's a good point, but Wes looks a lot better now..."

"Christian, I'm not discussing our friend's potential sex life with you right now. Get off my bed and go to sleep please."

:: ::

Entering *Downtown Beans,* Ash couldn't help but grin when he saw Brian's face drop when he saw him. The tall, beefy blond had been chatting with Camille behind the counter, but the moment Ash walked in, she'd come around to meet him with a deep kiss that he couldn't help prolonging for Brian's benefit.

"Coffee?"

"Please. I'm waiting for the boys. We're doing a group performance once they get out of school. Leah wants to post it online and is working us like dogs. I think I deserve a treat." He pouted at her, earning him another quick kiss before she slipped back behind the counter.

"You're loving every minute of it and you know it. So, don't pull the pout out on me."

"I am, and you love my pout," he teased, knowing it would create the blush to her skin that he adored.

"Shut up. I'm working."

Ash took his coffee and went to sit at his usual table to wait for Chris and Wes, pulling his ever-present journal out of his backpack. The moment he opened it to work on some lyrics that had been swimming around his head, everything around him melted away and it was just him and his music.

"Hey, music man, are you ready to please your audience?" Leah's voice jolted him out of his concentration, meaning he almost knocked over his stone-cold coffee.

"What audience?"

"The one you'll get while you all perform. You know it'll happen; it always does."

What had started for Ash as a way to generate some cash for the band, had quickly turned into a way to promote the band and the showcase now that Leah has become their unofficial manager and PR team all rolled up into one force of nature college student.

"Yeah, I'm just waiting for the guys. They've been on some field trip, so I didn't need to go and pick them up."

"They're here." Leah pointed over to the counter where Chris and Wes were both laughing and joking with Camille. He'd been so absorbed; he hadn't noticed them arrive.

"I guess I best get our gear out of the car then."

"Yeah, I guess you best."

With a grin, he bounced out of his seat, making sure his backpack was safe with Leah and made his way around to the lot where he'd parked his car. He slung his guitar case and Chris' bass over his shoulders before grabbing the mic stands and heading back to set up. Wes went with Chris to grab his cajon and the amps they needed while Ash fiddled with the mic stands. Eventually, they were ready, and Leah was standing on the sidewalk ready with her phone.

Trying to ignore the fact she was filming them – probably live on Instagram – the boys launched into Queen's *We Will Rock You,* which was not only a favorite of theirs, but tended to draw in a crowd. Chris and Ash started the stomp stomp clap that was iconic while Wes joined in on his cajon. Immediately, people walking past stopped to join in. As he sang, Ash could see Leah moving around recording them and the crowd. Judging by the wide smile on her face, they'd picked the right song to start with.

By the time Ash started in on his guitar solo - which always sounded better on his electric, but today the acoustic would have to do - the crowd was singing along and the guitar case was filling up with loose change and a few bills. When they finished, the applause was deafening.

"We're Rare Breed. Check us out at The Vine for our showcase." Leah appeared as Ash spoke into his mic, with a bunch of the posters to hand out which were grabbed at insanely quickly.

"Guys, that was inspired. It looks absolutely amazing on video. I'm going inside to connect to the Wi-Fi to post it everywhere." Leah was like a giddy schoolgirl as she ran inside. Without wasting any time, the guys began one of their own tracks, hoping to keep up the momentum and attention they were receiving.

For three hours straight, Rare Breed played music, handed out posters, and sold tickets to their showcase. By the time they were finished for the day, the three of them were drained and ready to just chill for the rest of the day. Wes swiftly disappeared to go and meet Wyatt from work, while Chris had more babysitting to do. Ash waited for Camille to finish her shift, then drove back to his house where they spent the rest of the day on his bed, wrapped up in one another's arms, talking about music and their lives in general, until they drifted off to sleep.

227

When Ash woke up, he realized he hadn't been so happy in a long time and the crushing in his chest hadn't been as prominent for a while. He knew it wouldn't go away completely, but it was easier to cope with. There was clearly something special about Camille Rogers, and he wasn't about to let her slip out of his fingers.

Working himself free of her sleeping grip, he made his way downstairs to make them both a coffee.

"Morning, honey." His mom brushed his shaggy hair from his face as she kissed his cheek.

"Morning, Mom." He grinned at her as he prepared the drinks, nothing unusual in itself as she was always so used to either Wes or Chris raiding her refrigerator for breakfast.

"When do I get to officially meet her?" she asked, bluntly.

"Uhm..."

Camille peeked from behind him. "Hi, Mrs. Kane. I'm Camille and it's nice to meet you."

28

Ash's heart was in his throat as he followed his dad's car, complete with borrowed trailer once again, to the venue. Hopefully, if they got a little more successful, they'd be able to purchase one of their own.

It was showcase day and he was ready to not only throw up, but to run away and never show his face again. He could give up music and go and become a surfer or something. Except he wasn't the strongest swimmer, and the ocean petrified him. After all, who *really* knew what was down there, hiding in the depths.

His heart rate began to spike, and he was starting to struggle to breathe.

"You okay?" Camille asked from the

passenger seat as she felt the car begin to slow down. Ash managed to find a space to pull over and open his door, needing air. He heard the passenger side door open, then close, and within seconds, Camille was crouched in front of him. "Hey, look at me. Breathe in.... and out. In through the nose, out through the mouth. Keep going... that's it."

As she pulled her phone out of her pocket, Ash could feel himself calming down, but the overwhelming urge to run was still there, and the pressure in his chest was growing. He concentrated on his breathing, leaning his head down so it was almost between his knees.

Ash tried to listen to what Camille was saying on the phone, but all he could hear was the odd word in between the whooshing sound in his head. It felt as if someone had held two seashells up to his ears.

"Hey, you're gonna be okay. Ash, look at me." Lifting his head felt like a chore, but he managed it and locked eyes with Camille. "It's all going to be okay."

"How do you know?" His voice was small, and he hated it. This was supposed to be a day for him to enjoy, to thrive on, but here he was

fighting off a panic attack in the middle of downtown L.A.

"Because I know *you*. And Wes, and Chris.
Together, you guys can overcome anything.
You're all insanely talented and this showcase is
just the beginning of what's to come." She kissed
him gently on his forehead as his breathing
slowly evened out. The two of them sat there, on
the side of the road in his beat-up old Chevy
until Ash could no longer feel his heart trying to
claw its way out of his throat.

"Thank you," he whispered as he wrapped
his arms around her.

"Thank me by slaying it on stage. Prove yourself wrong, prove to yourself that you *do* deserve
this, that you deserve to have people know who
you are and who feel things through your music."

Tears pricked at Ash's eyes as Camille spoke.
How was she able to see directly into the heart of
how he felt most days?

"I'll try, that's the best I can do."

"I'll take it. Now, let's get to that venue and
show Gabriel West what Rare Breed is all about."

:: ::

Their sound check went well, and once they'd got out of the venue for some air, Ash couldn't believe he'd almost run from the opportunity that was within his grasp. As he, Chris, and Wes took some time for just the three of them in the back streets of West Hollywood, Ash couldn't help but think about Joey. He'd been with them at the beginning of this crazy journey, and now they were making it on their own, without him.

"Hey, have you guys seen Joey around school much?" he asked.

"Not that I've noticed, why?" Wes responded, looking up from his phone.

"It's just that we always planned to do this with him, and now we're practically strangers. Feels weird is all."

"Well, that douche canoe is the reason we're a trio now. I've heard he's running with a new crowd and has been ditching school a lot."

"Well, his loss, eh, boys? Tonight is the start of the rest of our lives, and I for one couldn't imagine doing it without you two."

"Being in a relationship's made him go soft on us," Chris quipped, ducking out of the way of Ash's hand that aimed to slap him on the arm.

"Not too soft from what I've heard," Wes grinned.

"You fuckers. Maybe I should turn go solo?" Ash held his head in his hands, seriously questioning his choice of friends. Although, it had been clear to him for a long time that Wes and Chris were more than his friends, they were his family.

"You wouldn't last a week without us. Now, let's get back inside, Wyatt should be here soon."

The three of them walked back into the venue, arms wrapped around one another, jostling one another, and laughing. Life was good for Rare Breed at that moment in time, and Ash wanted it to last.

:: ::

As the lights dimmed, Ash looked out over the crowd that were cheering for them, he couldn't help but feel he was exactly where he needed to be. His journal had always been his escape, his way to hide away when the world around him felt too much. The words within were his way of making sense of everything that happened to him, to his friends, to their imme-

233

diate surroundings. Not all of them became songs and that was okay with Ash. Not everything needed to be molded into something else.

But the stage, the stage was his freedom from everything that had ever held him back. Whether it was a big venue like The Vine, or a street corner, he was always his true self when performing, and the crushing feeling in his chest didn't exist. All that mattered was the music and the reaction to it.

"We're Rare Breed," he announced, followed by a cheeky smile and a look back at both his friends. The crowd went wild.

As they took their final bow, with the crowd still going nuts for them, Ash managed to catch Camille's eye and winked at her. She'd helped him more than she'd ever know, and he'd make sure she knew she was appreciated.

Rare Breed left the stage and bounded back to their dressing room where they were soon a tangle of back slaps and hugs. It didn't take long for Camille, Wyatt, and Leah to join them. The six of them hooted and hollered until their voices were hoarse, but it didn't stop them.

Finally, they left the dressing room to meet up with other friends and family who had supported them at the showcase. Soon they were surrounded by many faces, both ones they knew and ones that were completely new.

"Dude, we're bonafide rock stars now," Chris hissed into his ear as he signed an autograph on one of the posters they'd been distributing for the past six weeks. Ash grinned at him, signing his own name.

Security soon came over to help move them from the crowd into the VIP area where Gabriel waited for them.

"Well, boys. I have to admit, I didn't think you'd pull it off, but here I am, suitably impressed."

"Thanks for the opportunity, Mr. West." Wes just had to be polite. None of them liked the guy, but he'd given them this evening.

"Great show, maybe you should consider taking up a residency here at The Vine?"

"Thanks, Mr. West, but no thanks. We're not a house band, but the offer's a great one and appreciated," Ash managed to respond without biting the guy's head off.

"The offer's always open, just in case." Gabriel turned to a small man standing behind him. "Boys, this is John Naismith, an agent with

BeachSide Talent. He'd like to have a word with you."

:: ::

By the time they got back to the garage, the high from the show was starting to wear off and Ash could feel the exhaustion of a come down starting to kick in. All he wanted to do was chill with the best people in his life, but Chris was still bouncing off the walls and counting the business cards they'd been handed. Ash hadn't expected too many music execs to show, but Gabriel had been true to his word.

"I don't think we should trust the guy Gabriel introduced us to. I feel it was his way of getting involved a bit too much," Wes commented.

"I agree, but we don't need to decide right now." Ash fell onto the couch, pulling Camille with him as Leah curled up at the other end. "For now, let's just bask in the legends we were on that stage."

"Guys, seriously, you were fantastic," Leah commented, looking sleepy.

"And we couldn't have done it without you." From behind the drumkit, Wes pulled out a huge bunch of flowers. "It's not much, but it's all we could do without you finding out."

Staring at them in shock for a while, Leah took the bouquet and tried not to cry.

"I'd do it all again, if you'll have me."

"Always."

EPILOGUE

Two Years Later:

It had been a long time since Ash and his friends had been part of an audience, but there was no way any of them would ever miss Camille and Leah's graduation. He, Chris, Wes, and Wyatt sat in a row near the front with Camille and Leah's families where they could see every inch of the stage.

They were still relatively unknown thanks to not taking a deal from any of the executives that had shown up at their showcase at The Vine. They'd decided to remain independent to have more control over their careers, and the only person they could ever imagine doing that with was Leah. She'd proved to them over and over that she was more than capable in booking them gigs and studio time. And she didn't take any shit from venue owners or managers. Having her in their corner was impressive and got them through doors.

They'd not long finished a small tour within California, but Ash knew that now Leah was finished with college, she was determined to set herself up with her own business that would look after not just Rare Breed, but the amazing song-writer Camille Rogers. None of them could imagine it any other way either.

Watching Camille walk across the stage to collect her diploma, Ash couldn't help the shout of pride escaping his lips, making everyone around him laugh.

"What?" he asked, schooling a look of inno-cence onto his face. Harry, Camille's dad, leaned over and gave him a high-five before making the same sound.

Then, it was Leah's turn. Their row went crazy for the girl who had not only become a friend, but the best thing that had happened to their careers. Unlike Camille, who had blushed and tried to hide her face, Leah held her head high and walked across the stage as if she owned it, a huge smile on her face.

Once the ceremony was over, and Harry had taken what felt like hundreds of photos, the group were free to hang out. Rather than go to a fancy restaurant like most graduates and their families, this family only had one place they wanted to be.

"You know, if it wasn't for this garage, there's no way on earth we'd be where we are right now," Chris commented as he slid onto the floor in front of the couch, leaning up against Leah's legs.

"Yeah, you would. You guys would have done it, just a bit slower," she responded as she ran her fingers through Chris' red hair, making him purr like a cat.

"Well, yeah. But you helped streamline it."

Ash watched them from across the room, wondering if they'd ever take the next step in their relationship. It had been a long time coming, but the two of them were completely oblivious. He smiled as Camille entered the garage, no longer in her cap and gown, but her diploma still in her hand. As she walked toward him, he couldn't ignore the pride blossoming in his chest where he now rarely felt the vice crushing him.

"Hey."

"Hey." She melted into his arms and he breathed in the aroma of her. The coffee was no longer present, but the coconut aroma of her shampoo was reassuring to him. Something familiar after the insane amount of changes he'd had to endure.

"Congratulations," he whispered as he pressed a kiss to her hair, feeling her body hum in pleasure at the minute amount of contact.

"Thank you. For being there, for being amazing, and for just, urgh, just for being you." Stretching up on her tiptoes, she kissed him.

"You never have to thank me for any of that. It's because of you I'm a better person."

Drawing her away from their friends a little more, Ash reached into his pocket and pulled out a box.

"Are you...?" Panic was written all over her face, making him chuckle. He'd considered it, but they were still far too young for all that. If he had his way, they had the rest of their lives together, but there was no rush to do anything. He just wanted them to enjoy being together, being a couple, being a partnership.

"No, I'm not proposing. Not yet at least." He nudged her. "Go on, open it."

A look of wonder soon replaced the panic as she saw the earrings. Delicate gold notes nestled in the box.

"They're beautiful."

"Just like you are, Camille Rogers, inside and out."

As Camille put them into her ears, Ash picked up his guitar. Chris was already at his side with his bass in his hands. It took Wes a while longer to join them, but once he did, he turned to Leah, Wyatt, Camille, and Ben, who had snuck in and sat on the back of the couch.

"You guys have been the best things to have happened to us three losers, and there's no way we'll ever be able to thank you for everything you've done for us, big or small. All we have is our music, the thing that brought us together."

"Ash, I swear, if you sing some 90s alt rock track, I'm leaving this garage and never coming back," Camille teased.

"Cam, would I do that to you?" He laughed at the resounding 'yes' that was thrown back at him by all of his friends. Before she could argue with him, he began the immediately recognizable intro riff of The Rembrandts *I'll Be There for You*.

The End

PLAYLIST

Green Day – Good Riddance (Time of Your
Life)
Nirvana – Come As You Are
Panic! At the Disco – The Ballad of Mona Lisa
Guns 'N' Roses – Sweet Child O' Mine
Green Day – Burnout
Weezer – Buddy Holly
The La's – There She Goes
5 Seconds of Summer – Old Me
Bon Jovi – You Give Love a Bad Name
Nirvana – Smells Like Teen Spirit
Green Day – Wake Me Up When September
Ends
Queen – We Will Rock You
The Rembrandts – I'll Be There for You

ACKNOWLEDGMENTS

Clare – You held my hand a lot through this one. So much appreciation heading your way. Thanks babe.

Dean 'thekingofwing' Roberts – Thanks for the info about showcases, it was invaluable, no matter what Stew says. Cheers pal.

Tammy – as ever you listen to what I ramble on about and come up with the most amazing covers and formatting. Thank you never seems to be enough to say.

Andie – You're a complete superstar and I adore you more than you know. We'll meet up, drink gin, and eat watermelon eventually. Your edits have been a Godsend.

Sarah – as always, here's your thanks. Thanks for

being you and supporting me for forever. You're my biscuit and I adore you, even if you refuse to join my new fandom.

My Inner Circle – You're all amazing with the constant support you've given me over the years. I love you all.

My Chowen group chat – ILY! Never forget that.

If I've forgotten anyone, please forgive me. This bit is nerve wracking as hell.

ABOUT THE AUTHOR

M. B. Feeney is an army brat who finally settled down in Birmingham, UK with her other half, two kids and a mini zoo. She often procrastinates by listening to music of all genres and trying to get 'just one more paragraph' written on whichever WIP is open; she is also a serious doodler and chocoholic.

Writing has been her one true love ever since she could spell, and publishing is the final culmination of her hard work and ambition. Her publishing career began with two novellas, and she currently has multiple projects under way, in the hopes that her portfolio of what have been described as "everyday love stories for everyday people" will continue to grow. Always having something on the go can often lead to block which eventually gets dissolved by good music and an even better book.

Her main reason for writing is to not only give her readers enjoyment, but also to create a story and characters that stay with readers long after the book is finished, and possibly make someone stop and think "what if... "

To keep up to date with her work and to see exclusive teasers of upcoming works, join her Facebook group

www.facebook.com/groups/feeneysinnercircle

or follow her on Instagram for an insight into her working life and living with her family and mini zoo

www.instagram.com/mbfeeneyauthor

BOOKS BY M. B. FEENEY

Right Click, Love

Just Like in the Movies

Honour

The One That Got Away

It Started in Texas

Looking Back from L.A.

Mile High

The Exchange Series

Girls and Boys

While You Were Asleep

Where There's a Will...

There She Goes

Her Best Friend's Brother

Masquerade

The Neighbour

Printed in Great Britain
by Amazon

82274854R00150